Horace C. Dale

Strife

an original comedy drama in four acts

Horace C. Dale

Strife
an original comedy drama in four acts

ISBN/EAN: 9783337343729

Printed in Europe, USA, Canada, Australia, Japan

Cover: Foto ©Andreas Hilbeck / pixelio.de

More available books at **www.hansebooks.com**

STRIFE

AN ORIGINAL COMEDY DRAMA IN FOUR ACTS

BY

HORACE C. DALE

AUTHOR'S EDITION CORRECTLY PRINTED FROM THE PROMPT
COPY, WITH THE ORIGINAL CAST OF THE CHARACTERS,
SYNOPSIS OF INCIDENTS, TIME OF REPRESENTATION,
DESCRIPTION OF THE COSTUMES, SCENE AND PROP-
ERTY PLOTS, DIAGRAMS OF THE STAGE SET-
TINGS, SIDES OF ENTRANCE AND EXIT,
RELATIVE POSITIONS OF THE PER-
FORMERS, AND ALL OF THE
STAGE BUSINESS.

NEW YORK
HAROLD ROORBACH
PUBLISHER

STRIFE.

———

CAST OF CHARACTERS.

———

Grand Opera House,
Reading, Pa.,
May 25th, 1887.

JUDGE HENRY BUTTONS, { *a retired Judge, and wealthy mill-owner.* }	Mr. William Ward.
HAROLD THOMAS, *a gentleman of leisure.*	Mr. Thomas Barrett.
HENRY HANSELL, *a mechanic.*	Mr. Horace C. Dale.
ARISTOTLE THOMPKINS, } *the Judge's most in-*	Mr. George R. Rice.
HORATIO SQUASH, } *timate friends.*	Mr. D. H. Purnell.
HANS VON SANDT, *his cook*	Mr. J. W. Lark.
JULIUS, } *his servants*	Mr. H. W. Buttons.
NEB, }	Mr. L. F. Welsh.
POLICEMAN, ...	Mr. William Bowen.
LAURA BELL, *the Judge's ward.*	Miss Claribel Lewis.
MRS. HANSELL, *Henry's mother.*	Miss Nina Monteith.
DOLLY, *a maid.*	Miss Clara Younge.
MARY HARRIS, ...	Miss Annie James.

MOB, *etc., by the company.*

THOMPKINS can be doubled and played by HANSELL; SQUASH by the POLICEMAN; and MARY by DOLLY.

———

TIME OF PLAYING.—TWO HOURS AND A QUARTER.

Time, the Present.   Locality, Wheeling, West Va.

SYNOPSIS OF INCIDENTS.

ACT I.—Reception-room in Judge Buttons' mansion.—An eavesdropper.—The Judge in a tantrum.—Guardian and ward.—"A frog he would a wooing go."—Some pointed observations.—The cause of humanity.—A timely warning.—"Go; and don't enter my house again unless I send for you!"—Echoes of the past.—A gentleman of leisure.—Mistaken identity.—Recognition.—An insult and a blow.—Threatened exposure.—Brought to bay.—A murderous assault.—A son's defence.—Humiliation.—Tableau.

ACT II, *Scene 1.* A street.—Julius goes "a-sparkin'."—Love at first sight.—Neb's peculiar method of "raising the wind."—Gentleman and workingman.—Rejection of proffered aid.—"Strike!"—"Lead on; I follow, to seal his fate!" *Scene 2.* Mrs. Hansell's home.—A mother's anxiety.—An excited visitor.—Welcome tidings.—Mother and son.—"Nobly spoken! Go, and may Heaven's blessing attend you." *Scene 3.* A street.—A villain's resolve.—Hans Von Sandt in the clutches of the law.—Neb in luck. *Scene 4.* Exterior of Judge Buttons' residence.—The mob's assault.—The mechanic's impassioned appeal.—Conflagration.—"Back, every man of you!"—Tableau.

ACT III.—The Judge's reception-room.—An embarrassing situation.—Hansell is sent for.—Good intentions, and an offered reward.—Some more pointed observations.—The workingman's ultimatum.—Reinstatement.—A question of duty.—An interruption.—A cowardly scheme.—Strange revelations.—The serpent's sting.—An interesting episode.—"Hail fellows, well met."—A slight unpleasantness in which Germany goes to the wall.—Tableau.

ACT. IV.—Same as before.—War declared against Hans.—A false attack.—Consternation.—The Judge secures his assailant.—Alienation.—A noble woman's defiance.—Indignation.—Accused of crime.—Impending disgrace.—A mother's intervention.—Villainy unmasked.—Foiled!—A great wrong righted.—"Nothing but sunshine."—Tableau.

COSTUMES.

JUDGE BUTTONS.—Black Prince Albert coat; black trousers; white vest; standing collar; black tie; patent leather shoes. Iron gray wig, side whiskers and moustache.

HAROLD THOMAS.—Act I. Prince Albert coat; black vest and trousers; patent leather shoes; white tie; standing collar; kid gloves; black wig and moustache.

Act II. Scenes 1 and 3, same as Act I, with silk hat. Scene 4, An old dark sack coat, vest and trousers; black felt hat pulled down over eyes.

Acts III and IV. Dress as per Act I.

HENRY HANSELL.—Act I. A neat dark sack coat, vest and trousers; light gray bicycle shirt; light four in-hand tie; neatly blackened shoes; dark derby hat, carried in hand; light wig and moustache.

Act II. Scenes 1 and 2, same as Act I. Scene 4, same as Act I, without coat and hat.

Acts III and IV.—Dress as per Act I.

HORATIO SQUASH.—Prince Albert coat; light plaid trousers; standing collar; white tie; rosebud in lapel of coat; half-bald white wig, and white throat whiskers.

ARISTOTLE THOMPKINS.—Prince Albert coat; dark vest and trousers; turn down collar; light silk cravat; half-bald gray-mixed wig; side whiskers and moustache of same color.

HANS.—Acts I, III and IV. White vest and trousers; white shirt and apron; paper cap; light crop wig.

Act II. Scenes 3 and 4, same as Act I, with linen duster and light felt hat.

POLICEMAN.—Double-breasted blue coat, vest and trousers; light helmet, star and club.

JULIUS.—Acts I, III and IV. Linen sack coat, vest and trousers; percale shirt and collar; negro wig.

Act II. Scenes 1 and 3. Black cutaway coat; light plaid trousers; white vest; silk hat; light kid gloves; standing collar; broad red tie; heavy gaudy watch chain; fancy cane. Scene 4. Same, without hat.

NEB.—Acts I and IV. Linen sack coat, dark vest and trousers; percale shirt and collar, negro wig.

Act II. Scene 1. Bright, large-figured calico dress; broad summer hat with red trimmings; red bow at throat; immense high bustle; fan attached at belt with red ribbon.

Scenes 2 and 4. Same as in Act I, with soft felt hat.

Scene 3. Dress as per Act I, with hat. Policeman's disguise over clothes—see description.

Act III. Light checkered trousers; black cutaway coat and vest; white shirt; immense standing collar; cuffs; red tie.

LAURA.—Act I. A handsome tea gown. Blonde wig.

Act II. Scene 2. A fashionable street dress; kid gloves; summer hat.

Scene 4. White evening dress, trimmed with lace; low neck, short sleeves; jewelry.

Act III. Black lace and amber dress.

Act IV. A cream colored décolleté reception gown, with train.

MRS. HANSELL.—Act II. A plain black house dress; iron gray wig.

Act IV. Black street dress; black bonnet and gloves; heavy black veil.

DOLLY.—Acts I and IV. A plain light house dress; white apron; chestnut wig.

Act III. Same as Act I, with the addition of a dusting cap.

MARY.—Night dress; light girlish wig.

MOB.—Red, blue and gray flannel shirts; sleeves partly rolled up; shabby trousers; rough boots; hats of various textures, shapes and colors; hands and faces begrimed; general appearance repulsive.

PROPERTY PLOT.

ACT I.—Furniture as per scene plot. Table cover. Call bell. Dish and cut flowers. Magazines. Vases for organ. Sheet music. Three rugs. Easels and paintings. Whip. Pistol. Dagger.

ACT II.—Cane. Seven silver dollars. Handcuffs. Lamp. Bible. Pitcher, and one tumbler. Basket. $4.50 in silver. Stuffed billy. Money for Thomas. Coffee sack for Neb. Two bags of shavings for fagots. Coal oil barrel. Conflagration pot. Gun. Pistol. Coverlet for couch. Furniture as per scene plot.

ACT III.—Dust pan, brush and rag. Waiter. Two bottles of wine. (weak tea to represent wine) Three wine glasses. Three bottles for Julius. One demijohn. Cane. Bladder for Hans.

ACT IV.—Letter for Laura. Two putty blowers. Two bladders. Flour for Hans. Pistol, loaded, for Judge. Cleaver and gun. Letter for Hansell. Horse pistol for Julius. Dagger for Thomas. Pistol, loaded, for property man.

STAGE SETTINGS.

Acts I, III and IV.

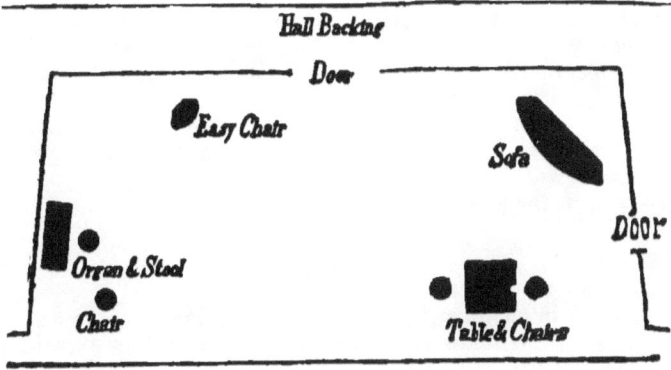

Act II—*Scene 2.*

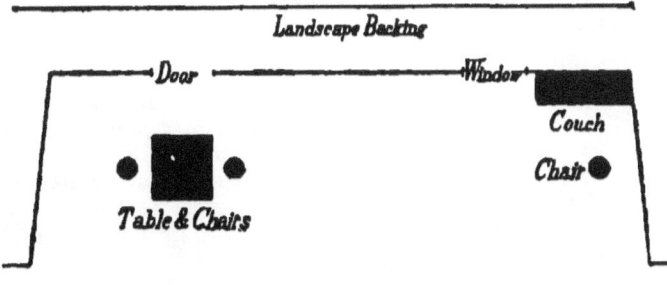

Act II—*Scene* 4.

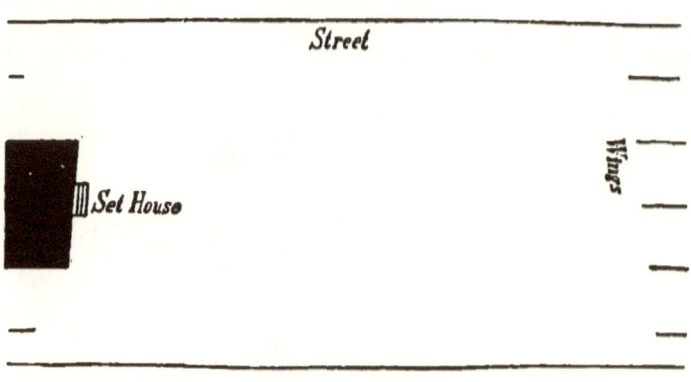

Street

Set House

Wings

SCENE PLOT.

Acts I, III and IV.

Reception-room in Judge Buttons' mansion. Fancy chamber boxed in
4 G., backed with hall or corridor backing in 5 G. Practicable door L. 2
E. Practicable double or folding doors C., in flat. Table L. C., opposite
L. I E., with chairs R. and L. of it. Another chair down R., and easy
chair up R. C. Open cabinet organ, with stool, across R. 2 E. Sofa across
extreme upper L. corner, leaving sufficient room for NEB to get behind
sofa. Carpet down. Lights up. In ACT IV the lights are to be lowered
and flashed up at the prompter's signal.

Act II.

SCENES I and 3.—Street in I G.
SCENE 2.—Plain chamber in 3 G., backed with landscape in 4 G. Practicable door R. F. Window L. F. Common square table R. C., with chairs
R. and L. of it. Chair at L. 2 E. Couch up L.
SCENE 4.—A street in 5 G. Set house, with practicable door and steps,
across R. 2 E. and R. 3 E. The scene on the flat represents a continuation
of the street on which the house is situated. In the L. background are
seen the blazing ruins of Judge Buttons' mill. Sky illumined. Lights
low throughout.

STAGE DIRECTIONS.

In observing, the player is supposed to face the audience. R. means
right; L., left; C., centre; R. C., right of centre; L. C., left of centre; D.
F., door in the flat or back scene; R. F., right side of the flat; L. F., left
side of the flat; R. D., right door; L. D., left door; C. D., centre door; I
E., first entrance; 2 E., second entrance; U. E., upper entrance; I, 2 or 3
G., first, second or third grooves; UP STAGE, toward the back; DOWN
STAGE, toward the foot-lights.

R.   R. C.   C.   L. C.   L.

STRIFE.

ACT I.

Scene.—*Reception-room in* JUDGE BUTTONS' *mansion, luxuriously furnished—table, covered, with call bell, books and cut flowers on it—vases of cut flowers on organ top—sheet music on rack—skin or Persian rugs under table, at organ and at sofa—handsome paintings on easels around room—*JULIUS *kneeling with hands clasped, down* C., *crying—*DOLLY *standing over him, enraged, with uplifted riding whip—curtain rises to lively music.*

Julius. (*sobbing*) P-l-e-a-s-e don't! I'll n-e-b-b-e-r, *neb-ber* tell on yo' ag'in!

Dolly. (*with warmth*) Will you promise always to call me *Miss* Dolly hereafter?

Julius. Yes—yes—mum.

Dolly. And you pledge yourself never to listen again at the key-hole when Miss Laura and I are talking privately?

Julius. No, mum, dat I'll nebber do ag'in.

Dolly. You won't *repeat* anything you hear to that Mr. Thomas? (JULIUS *hesitates*) You won't answer, eh? (*makes feint as though to strike* JULIUS *with whip*)

Julius. (*quickly*) No, no, mum, 'deed and *double*' deed I won't!

Dolly. Swear it, then.

Julius. (*expostulating*) Miss Dolly, I'se don't know how. Dis child nebber swore in his life.

Dolly. What! Do you forget what I heard you saying to Neb last night? Now I think it about time you were taught to have some regard for the truth, so prepare yourself for your first lesson. (*starts to slightly roll up right sleeve, talking the while*) Now say your prayers!

Julius. "Now I lay me down to sleep—" (*breaking off abruptly*) Oh, Miss Dolly, I 'spects I can do it. It hab just cum to me.

(*slightly raises index finger of right hand and speaks solemnly*) I'se
swear nebber to tell nuthin'——

Dolly. (*interrupting*) Anything!

Julius. (*quickly correcting himself*) *Anything* dat I don't hear——

Dolly. (*quickly*) *Do* hear!

Julius. Do hear to dat Mr. Thomas, no matter what it am.

Dolly. That will do. Now remember that oath and don't you
ever let me catch you at any of your badness again, (*going*) for if
you *do*, this will not be a circumstance to what you will receive
next time.   **Exit** C. D.; *takes whip with her.*

Julius. (*rising and talking to audience*) If eber she catches dis
chile ag'in in such a ticklish situation as she did dis mornin', den
I'se don't know hisself. She t'inks dat I took de oath, (*laughs*)
but I didn't, kase yo' mus' kiss de Bible or hold up yo' hand dis
way—(*elevates right arm to fullest extent*) to swear, an' I'se only
raised dis finger. (*chuckles to self*) She can't git ahead ob dis son
ob "Old Nick," as de Judge calls me. I jest 'spects dat Neb
done went and laid Miss Laura's riding-whip on dat table (*points
to table*, L.) on purpose. He's de meanest black niggar dat eber
I seed, and Dolly is de wustest poor white trash ob a gal dat eber
wus born. So I'se not to listen at de keyhole any more? Nor
tell Massa Thomas what I hear? We'll see! As long as dat man
treats me to dese fellahs (*displays silver dollars*) he can count on
Julius' influence at de court whar de Judge presides. Dat Dolly
'siders herself de boss of dis abode of Justice. (DOLLY *is seen softly
entering* C. D., *stands a moment near door, then quietly approaches
back of* JULIUS) She puts on more airs dan de Judge hisself. (*contemptuously*) Call her *Miss!* I'll see her in Guinea fust.

As JULIUS *stops speaking,* DOLLY *catches him by coat collar with her
left hand, boxing him terrifically over ear with her right—*NEB
peeps in from C. D., *and seems fairly wild with joy at* JULIUS' *pre-
dicament.*

Dolly. (*boxing him vigorously*) So, you won't "*miss*" me, eh?

Julius. (*ducking and trying to break away*) Yes, I will; 'deed
I will, *Miss* Dolly. I wus no 'ferring to yo'. I meant dat Dolly
who brings us de milk. Oh, Lor', Lor', what shall I do? (*dances
and howls*)

Dolly. (*still boxing him*) I guess you forgot some one else could
listen at door cracks besides yourself. Take that, and *that* and
THAT!

Julius. (*howls*) Oh, oh, oh!

Dolly. Now then—(*gives him an extra cuff and releases him*) go
and attend to your duties, (*goes toward* C. D.—NEB *quickly disappears as he sees* DOLLY *turn*) and *mind*, don't you let me see you
here when I return.

          Exit C. D., *with spirit, and slams it after her.*

Julius. (*rubbing ears and wiping tears from eyes*) Darn her picture! I'll paralyze her yet.

Enter NEB, C. D., *stands near door.*

Neb. (*affecting surprise*) Why, Jule, what's de mattah?
Julius. None ob yo' bis'ness, yo' mean, black niggah, yo'!
Neb. (*assuming a threatening attitude*) Who's yo's a-callin' a black niggah, hey? Does yo' want me to knock de blackin' off b dat ole skillet ob yourn ag'in?
Julius. (*slightly recedes, speaks quickly*) No, no; but what fur o' lebe dat ridin'-whip ob Miss Laura's in dis room?
Neb. (*aside*) Oh, ho, I see! (*to* JULIUS) Say, Jule, wus dat yo' heard hollerin' so a moment ago?
Julius. No, it wasn't!
Neb. Who wus it den?
Julius. I dunno.
Neb. Wusn't Dolly a lickin' ob yo's?
Julius. (*affecting surprise*) Dolly a-lickin' ob me? I guess not, n' she'd better not try it, neider.
Neb. Why, I seed her wid my own eyes.
Julius. Whar wus yo'?
Neb. Lookin' at yo' thro' de door dar! (*points to* C. D.)
Julius. (*confidentially*) I say, Neb, I'll gib yo' a pinter, if yo' in keep it to yo'self. When anybody is a-lickin' ob yo', jest holler out like as if dey wus a murderin' ob yo' an' den yo'll not git urt.
Neb. (*looks at him a moment*) So dat is de way yo' does, am it?
Julius. Ebbery time.
Neb. Den *yo'* wus a playin' 'possum an' I didn't hurt yo' last ight when I lammed yo' in de hoss trough. (*advances angrily pon* JULIUS *who appears uneasy and slowly backs toward sofa*)
Julius. (*alarmed*) Yes, yo' did. I wus not 'ludin' to dat kind b a lickin'.
Neb. Yes, yo' wus too, an' now I 'tend to do yo' up brown. *strikes* JULIUS *who falls backward upon sofa; gets on top of him, nd proceeds to pummel him lively; protesting voices mingle*) Don't o' holler, kase if yo' do I'll murder yo'. (*work scene up well*)
Julius. (*trying to throw* NEB *off*) Don't, don't, Nebby, yo're a motherin' ob me. Git off quick, I'se most dead.
Judge. (*calling off,* L. 2 E.) Julius! Neb! You Julius!
Julius. Dar's Massa comin' in! (NEB *jumps up quickly and runs ut* C. D., *followed by* JULIUS—NEB *closes door and prevents* JULIUS, *ho is thoroughly frightened, from leaving the room—tries door and peaks beseechingly*) Oh, Nebby, please let me out. (NEB *opens oor just wide enough to allow his grinning face to be seen, then loses it again*)
Judge. (*calling off,* L. 2 E.) You Julius! You Neb!

JULIUS *seems frantic with fear, tries door again, seems undecided, but finally darts behind sofa*—JUDGE enters *in a towering passion,* D. L. 2 E., *looks around room and goes to table.*

Judge. Not *here* either! (*taps call bell angrily several times in rapid succession, walks across front excitedly, talking*—JULIUS *watches him from behind sofa and appears immensely tickled*) Confound it! Plague take these easy-going, independent, *infernal* servants! Here I have one for nearly every room in the house, yet they are never within calling distance when wanted. (*taps bell viciously*) Hang it! I'd drown or murder in cold blood every mother's son of them, if I only dared. Why don't some one come? I shall go frantic! (*goes to* C. D., *and calls*) Neb! Julius! Hans! Dolly! (*returns to table talking, stands back of it and vigorously plies bell*) Just let me lay my hands on those black apes. (JULIUS' *head is seen above sofa back, grinning*) I'll make them remember this morning 'till their dying hour. (JULIUS *comes from behind sofa and stands erect,* C., *appearance of having just entered the room*—*The* JUDGE, *as bell stops ringing, passes around* L. *of table toward footlights*) That ought to be sufficient to awaken and summon the slumbering spirits of Hades.

Julius. (*innocence itself*) Did yo' ring, sah?

Judge. (*looks at him a moment, and then in a burst of passion*) Did yo' ring, sah? Did yo' ring, sah? (*starts for* JULIUS *who evades him*) I'll *wring* your black neck for you when I lay my hands upon you. (*as he reaches* C. D., NEB *enters hastily*)

Neb. (*speaking as he enters*) Did yo' ring, sah? (*the* JUDGE *turns furiously upon* NEB—*they collide,* NEB *falls*—JULIUS *down* R.)

Judge. (*kicking the prostrate form of* NEB *who rolls over and over*) Where have you been? I've been ringing the last hour and a half. (*turns* R., *and starts for* JULIUS—NEB *rises and goes down* L., *limping and rubbing himself*—enter DOLLY, L. D., *speaks the instant she enters*)

Dolly. Were you ringing, sir?

Judge. (*up* R.; *throws up both hands with horror depicted upon countenance*) Heaven preserve me! (*turns as though to leave room hurriedly*)

Enter HANS, *hurriedly,* C. D.

Hans. Vas dot you ring—(*seeing the* JUDGE *furiously advancing upon him, he turns quickly to* exit, *but the* JUDGE *gives him a violent kick as he leaves the room*)

Judge. (*slightly advancing* C., *greatly excited, imitates* HANS) Vos dot you ring? Go to the devil, every one of you! (DOLLY *tosses head and* exits, L. D., *slamming it after her*—NEB *stands still*—JULIUS *starts* C. D., *but is halted just in front of the* JUDGE *by his commanding tone*)

Judge. (*to* JULIUS) Where are you going?

Julius. (*terribly frightened, trembles and stammers*) I wus goin'—comin' to de *debbil.*

Judge. (*grabs him and shakes him furiously*) You were *coming* to the *devil*—to ME, you black rascal, were you! (*cuffs him on ear and kicks him out* C. D.; *then walks down* R. *very excitedly*) Was ever mortal so tried before, by a lot of block-headed servants? I really hardly know whether I am myself or not. I'm in a passion. I know I am, but how could one keep cool under such exasperating circumstances? (*sees* NEB) Neb!

Neb. Sah!

Judge. Who made my tea this morning?

Neb. Why, Hans, Massa.

Judge. Go send him to me this instant.

Neb. Yes, Massa. Exit C. D.

Judge. (*crossing to table, takes seat* L.) My breakfast ruined! A morning's pleasure destroyed! My amiable disposition soured all on account of the incompetence, stupidity and indifference of my servants, who seem to run this house to suit *their* inclinations, while *I*—(*bitterly*) *I* enjoy the exquisite pleasure of paying them for the privilege!

Enter NEB *followed by* HANS *who pauses at threshold, looks* R. *and* L., *but* enters *boldly when he perceives the position of the* JUDGE—*stands* C., NEB *by his* R.

Judge. (*angrily to* HANS) What did you do to my tea you made for breakfast?

Hans. Vot vos de matter mit dot tay?

Judge. I could not drink the vile stuff. Ugh! It tasted like a mixture of salts and senna.

Hans. Dot tay vos goot. Dere vos noddings de matter mit it.

Judge. (*sternly*) There *was*, I tell you. What do you mean by standing there and contradicting *me*? Do you think me bereft of the sense of *taste?* Don't you suppose I am able to distinguish the difference in taste between tea and—and—good whiskey?

Hans. Any von dot knows you, knows dot!

Judge. (*irritated*) What do you mean? Knows what?

Hans. Dot you vos von good whiskey judge!

Judge. (*picks up call bell*) You infernal——

Neb. (*quickly interrupting*) Massa, I 'spects dat Hans got hold ob de senna caddy, 'stead ob de tea, an' dat sumbody put salt in de sugar bowl. I seed Julius a-meddlin' wid dose tings early dis mawnin'.

Judge. I suppose Julius' interference will account for the eggs being fried in sweet oil, and the gravy being seasoned with sugar and emery sand, too, will it?

Hans. (*emphatically*) Dot *gravy* vos all right.

Judge. (*nettled*) How do you know?

Hans. I tasted it mine self.

Judge. (*horrified*) You tasted it?

Hans. Yah.

Judge. In what manner?

Hans. Mid de spoon.

Judge. The one you were stirring it with?

Hans. Yah.

Judge. (*rising, speaks angrily*) Have you the impudence to stand there and tell *me* that you *taste* articles of food intended for *my* table before sending them in?

Neb. Why, Massa, all good cooks taste ebery t'ing 'fore sendin' dem in, to see if dey is all right.

Judge. (*to* NEB) Hold your tongue, you imp of Satan! (*ludicrous attempt of* NEB *trying to literally hold his tongue—*JUDGE *goes back of table,* NEB *and* HANS *slowly backing*) Get out of my sight, both of you, quick, or you will soon be fit subjects for an undertaker. (*the* JUDGE *walks excitedly toward them—*HANS *and* NEB *frightened, break for* C. D.; NEB *trips and falls—*HANS *falls heavily upon him.* NEB *screams in abject terror*)

Neb. Mercy, Massa, mercy! (HANS *quickly springs to his feet, darts a startled look over his shoulder at the* JUDGE *and runs out* C. D., *followed by* NEB—*the* JUDGE *is excitedly pacing stage and does not notice the collision*)

Judge. What is the world coming to? To have one's food sampled—*tasted*—before it is set before him! Ugh! It is enough to irritate a saint, and make him sigh for a resting-place amid the suburbs of Paradise!

Enter LAURA, L. D.; *she stands a moment in astonishment, looking at the* JUDGE.

Laura. Why, what is the matter, sir?

Judge. (*cooling down*) Nothing, my dear, that is, nothing of particular importance. I have just been trying to obtain a solution of a mystery from my servants. But be seated, my dear. (*places chair* R. *of table and occupies the one* L—*looks at her fondly*) Your early rising, combined with your daily habit of riding is fast bringing back the roses to your cheeks.

Laura. Do you really think so? I am so glad, for you know how fond I am of your approbation.

Judge. (*aside*) Yes, I know you are, you sly puss. (*aloud*) You are positively becoming pretty. I fear it will not be long ere some gallant knight will come along and want to carry off *my* treasure as his prize.

Laura. Never fear on that score. I am too well satisfied to be with you, and love you too dearly to sever the pleasant relationship existing between us at present.

Judge. (*to audience, rubbing hands, and manifesting pleasure*) She *loves* me ! (*elevates eyebrows*) I have known it all along.

Laura. You are the only father I ever knew and I am sure my own could not have been kinder to me than you have been.

Judge. No doubt of it, no doubt of it, my child.

Laura. There has not been a wish of mine you have left unsatisfied thus far, and I feel at a loss how to testify my gratitude.

Judge. Tut ! tut ! You must not think of such matters. I have only done my duty to my dying friend, your father, who left you in my care. Providence will yet open a way for you to attest your love. (*aside*) Now if I could only muster up courage I would propose to her right away. *I know* she would accept me, for *she loves me!*

Laura. I sincerely trust so, and that I may not be found lacking in those noble attributes of woman, *devotion* and *love.*

Judge. (*aside*) Now is your chance ! Oh, for a little of my boyish nerve ! (*aloud, nervously*) You say you love me ?

Laura. Most devotedly.

Judge. (*aside*) That's encouraging ! (*aloud*) Have always done so ?

Laura. Ever since I learned to talk and *you* taught me what love was.

Judge. (*aside—gleefully rubs hands*) Better yet. (*aloud*) And that you will always continue to do so?

Laura. As long as I live and retain your memory.

Judge. (*aside—smiling*) Was ever man so blest before? She literally *forces* a declaration from me. (*aloud*) Will you never allow another to usurp my position in your heart's affection?

Laura. (*firmly*) Never ! for it is too deeply imbedded therein.

Judge. (*aside, immensely tickled*) Now, watch for her exhibition of gratitude and behold her lovely arms encircling her guardian's neck, while her melodious voice whispers, "*I am thine, forever!*" (*aloud, clears throat*) Laura, I think it about time you were married.

Laura. (*rises and stands* R. *of table*) Oh, please, sir, don't send me away from you just now !

Judge. (*aside*) She's mine beyond question ! (*aloud*) Who said anything about sending you away? I mean you ought to be settled in life—provided with a husband.

Laura. (*nervously*) But—but—I don't want to be married just yet.

Judge. (*aside*) She thinks I don't know she's in love with me, and that I wish to banish her from my presence. Sly rogues, these young girls ! (*aloud—reassuringly*) Of course not, there's no hurry. But I thought it advisable to tell you, (*fairly beams upon her*) that I know some one who loves *you*—fairly dotes upon you—and wants to marry you, too.

Laura. (*aside*) Could Henry have been so unwise as to disclose his sentiments toward me?

Judge. And you love him, too. (*raises right hand in playful, warning manner, smiling*) Now don't attempt to deny it!

Laura. How did you guess my secret?

Judge. (*laughing*) Oh, you innocent rogue! I saw it in your eyes. (*affectionately*) You could not conceal it from me.

Laura. You will consider what you have discovered in the light of confidence, won't you?

Judge. Oh, certainly, my dear. Until you are ready to name the wedding-day I shall not breathe a word of this to a living soul. I am so happy! I wish I were a boy again and at liberty to give vent to my exuberance of spirits.

Laura. (*smiling*) And I am so glad you approve of my choice, and that *I* have *made* you happy.

Judge. (*rising*) You are a noble girl! The very image of the one I have oft seen in my dreams, whom fate decreed should bless with her sweet smile my declining years. When we are near——

Re-enter NEB C. D., *followed by* HENRY HANSELL.

Neb. (*bowing*) A gem'man to see de Judge. (*stands up* R.)

Laura. (*to* JUDGE) Excuse me, sir. With your permission I will retire. (*goes to* L. D., *and glances at* HANSELL *as she* exits)

Judge. (*takes seat at table* L.—*a hard cold repulsive expression replaces the smiling tenderness of his features—*NEB *slips behind sofa as* HANSELL *advances* C.—JUDGE *toys with bell but speaks sarcastically*) To what am I *indebted* for the honor of this visit?

Hansell. The cause of humanity, sir.

Judge. Meaning, I presume, that you have been sent as a committee of one by the members of Celestial Union, No. 14, to present me with a testimonial extolling my many virtues and expressive liberal warm-heartedness in being the instrument that has caused misery, pestilence and want to bloom where heretofore the flowers of health, happiness and plenty were wont to flourish!

Hansell. I am very sorry to find that you feel so bitterly toward your men. I had hoped that the breech was not so wide, but even yet it might be bridged over.

Judge. Never! The chasm is too wide and too deep for my men and myself to shake hands across. Either *they* or *I* must go down its yawning abyss. Only yesterday your committeemen told me *I* was starving their wives and little ones, and that *I* was accountable for *all* their sufferings the past six months. I have been branded as a bloated capitalist, accused of being devoid of feeling and a worthy subject for a hangman's knot. And for what? Because competition and a dullness of trade prohibited me from acceding to their demanded increase of wages.

Hansell. But you forget that your men offered to return and resume work at their old wages.

Judge. No, I do not. Neither do I forget that the season's trade was *ruined* before that kind offer was made me. Now that my men *are* out, they can remain there until they agree to *my* conditions and sign my articles.

Hansell. (*with warmth*) *That* they will never do! The death-knell of slavery was sounded years ago, and the chains of serfdom which fell clanging from the limbs of their imprisoned victims, will ne'er re-echo through the realms of this free country, until the blue vault of heaven above us is rent in twain and the heart of man proves false to its own best interest!

Judge. (*emphatically*) Then, sir, my mill remains closed.

Hansell. But, sir——

Judge. (*interrupting*) You have heard my final decision. Entreaties are useless.

Hansell. Listen to me but one moment——

Judge. Not a word——

Hansell. (*quickly*) But you *shall!*

Judge. (*rising quickly and speaking angrily*) Do you dare?

Hansell. (*quickly*) Ay, I *dare* anything when the lives of human beings are in jeopardy. You do not understand the temper of your men, nor their vindictiveness, else you would be more reasonable. I came here to warn you that your life and property are in great danger.

Judge. You were sent here to threaten me, you mean.

Hansell. No, sir. I came of my own free will. Were my fellow workmen aware of my mission here, my life would not be worth two straws.

Judge. (*significantly*) So you risk your life in my behalf, do you? (*sneeringly*) What a noble exhibition of heroism!

Hansell. When threats are *openly* made against the life and property of a fellow being, a *man* would disgrace his Maker did he refrain from warning him of his danger, even though he *be* his most bitter enemy.

Judge. (*sarcastically*) Thank you, my *friend.* I am deeply sensible of the debt of gratitude I owe you, and (*sneeringly*) also of the motives governing your actions.

Hansell. I have done but my duty—less I could not do. I desire no ill to befall you——

Judge. (*quickly interrupting and closely watching the effect of his words*) Nor my ward and presumed heiress, Laura Bell!

Hansell. *She* has nothing to do with the case!

Judge. Hasn't she? Do you expect *me* to believe that?

Hansell. (*with warmth*) You are at liberty to *believe* what you please, and put whatever construction you see fit upon my motives, as long as *I* know them to be pure.

Judge. (*trembling with passion*) Hark ye, Mr. Highstrung Hansell, I am aware of your presumptuous aspirations and secret intrigues for the heart and hand of my ward, but *never, sir,* NEVER, shall *she* be the wife of a low born, arrogant, poverty-stricken wretch like yourself.

Hansell. Poverty, sir, is no disgrace—and that reminds me—that the mantle of true gentlemanliness is more frequently found in the homes of the lowly of our land, than among the wealthy who dwell in gilded palaces.

Judge. (*goes slightly back of table*) You forget, sir, where you are and *whom* you are addressing.

Hansell. (*quickly*) No, sir, I do not.

Judge. (*sneeringly*) *You* are but a common mechanic——

Hansell. (*interrupting*) And *you?*

Judge. A wealthy, educated *gentleman!*

Hansell. Nature draws no distinction between the two.

Judge. (*amazed*) What! Do you consider *our* social positions the same? *You* the offspring of *hirelings*, and *I* the descendant of culture, refinement and wealth?

Hansell. In the eyes of Nature all men are *born* equal, *die* equal and have a common hereafter.

Judge. (*slightly advances toward* HANSELL, *laboring under excitement; speaks significantly*) In the eyes of Nature some men are *born* fools, while *others make* fools of *themselves.*

Hansell. (*significantly*) Equally is it that the cloak of wealth, culture and refinement is oft used as a disguise to conceal the mean, grasping, unrelenting disposition of the being it envelopes!

Judge. (*in a passion*) Get out of my house, this instant; your language and insinuations are unbearable, sir! (HANSELL *hesitates*; JUDGE *points to* C. D. *as he advances*) Go, and don't you enter my house again, unless I send for you! (**exit** HANSELL C. D.) His manner and language was *offensive, very* offensive, yet—(*thoughtfully—soft music*) his independence of spirit I cannot help admiring, while his appearance suggested a superior order of being. Of whom does he remind me? Features, spirit, address, *all* suggest some familiar one of the dim past. When e'er I see him, his vision haunts me for days and racks my brain with conflicting emotions, as the barriers of the Past are torn down and their scenes re-enacted. Oh, for the power to obliterate from memory the scenes of my younger days! (*assumes naturalness*) But why allow the vision of a *mere mechanic* to distract me? 'Tis childish! I will order some wine and dispel these unpleasant thoughts. (*music ceases—starts for table* L.)

Re-enter JULIUS L. D., *followed by* THOMAS.

Julius. Mr. Thomas to see yo,' sah. (*bows and* exits L. D.)

Judge. (*pleasantly*) Good morning, Mr. Thomas, good morning, sir. (*shakes hand and offers him a seat* R.) I am happy to see you. Take a seat.

Thomas. Thank you. I suppose you are aware of my object in visiting you this morning, as you received my note last evening?

Judge. (*seated at table*) Yes, sir, and I assure you I appreciate your meditated honor—but——

Thomas. (*quickly*) I hope you will raise no objection to my honorable proposition. I am aware you have known me but a short time, yet my letters of introduction——

Judge. (*interrupting*) Were all right. I have no objection to your paying attentions to my ward—none at all, and if you win her heart I will gladly give my consent to your union—only——

Thomas. Only what?

Judge. (*pauses*) Only I consider your case hopeless.

Thomas. Why?

Judge. I have every reason for thinking her affections are centered upon another.

Thomas. (*eagerly*) Whom?

Judge. (*smiling*) Well—really—I—I—you must excuse me. I am not at liberty to tell you.

Thomas. There must be a mistake. I really can't believe it! Can I see Miss Bell?

Judge. (*rising*) Certainly, and if you will excuse me, I will call her myself. Exit, L. D.

Thomas. (*rises, comes* R. C.) I cannot believe the Judge is right in his suspicion, or else Laura is a most consummate coquette! (*thoughtfully*) I wonder who it is the Judge thinks has won her affections.

Re-enter HANSELL, C. D.—*speaks as he enters.*

Hansell. Judge, I—(*starts as he perceives* THOMAS) I beg your pardon, I thought *you* were the Judge!

Thomas. (*aside*) Here may be a solution of the mystery. (*to* HANSELL ; *speaks as he advances*) So we have met at last, in spite of your artful dodging!

Hansell. I do not understand you.

Thomas. Don't you? What business have *you* to enter this room as though you were lord and master here?

Hansell. That is an affair of my own and does not concern you.

Thomas. (*at* HANSELL'S R. *side*) Don't it though? Perhaps you pretend not to recognize me?

Hansell. (*with dignity*) Truly can I answer, *I do not !*

Thomas. And in doing it, you add another falsehood to your already long category of sins.

Hansell. (*angrily*) You lie!

Thomas. What's that?

Hansell. I presume you understood me, I spoke plainly enough.

Thomas. (*angrily*) Yes, too plainly—take that. (*slaps* HANSELL'S *face*) and let it be a warning to you to be more choice in the selection of epithets in the future, when you address a *gentleman.*

Hansell. (*restraining his passion*) A *gentleman*, sir, would disdain to abuse the hospitality of his host and be guilty of *your* contemptible action. I shall not attempt to resent it *here.*

Thomas. (*sneeringly*) No! nor anywhere else, you cowardly cur.

Hansell. We shall meet again where the courtesies of society do not prohibit a man from *resenting* an insult.

Thomas. (*coolly*) As you please ; I waive all rights. Let it be shotguns at ten paces, pistols at five, or knives face to face. It is all the same to me.

Hansell. You shall hear from me in a few days.

Thomas. The *sooner*, the better. Now I wish to know whether the rumor be true, that you aspire to be the husband of Miss Bell.

Hansell. I decline to answer your impertinent question.

Thomas. (*angrily*) I demand an answer!

Hansell. (*coolly*) You do, eh? Pray, upon what grounds?

Thomas. That if you refuse, I'll reveal to the Judge and Miss Bell——

Hansell. (*quickly interrupting*) You are then——

Thomas. The *gentleman* who knows a chapter of your past that would not be well for *you* to have related to the Judge and Miss Bell.

Hansell. (*quickly*) You surely would not attempt to injure me—

Thomas. (*interrupting*) Build not a castle of hopes upon my generosity.

Hansell. (*bitterly*) No fear of that. I know you too well ever to expect anything at your hands, but treachery and deceit.

Thomas. (*advancing, enraged*) What's that?

Hansell. (*threateningly*) Be careful! Don't attempt to repeat your insult, or *I* may forget where *I* am and resent it.

Thomas. Do you refuse to answer my question?

Hansell. I do!

Thomas. (*down* R. HANSELL C.) Then I'll reveal to the Judge your true character.

Hansell. Well?

Thomas. Communicate to Miss Bell your crime.

Hansell. No doubt of it!

Thomas. Publish to the world the perjury committed by your sister and——

Hansell. (*passionately*) Stop! Don't you dare cast reflections upon my mother and sister.

Thomas. (*quickly*) You know what they did, and I will.

Hansell. (*with power*) No, you won't, not while I am living to protect them. *They* swore to what they considered to be true, while *you* tried to place a halter around an innocent man's neck.

Thomas. 'Tis false!

Hansell. It is true, and you will yet suffer for *your* folly.

Thomas. (*slightly agitated*) What do you mean?

Hansell. (*watching him*) Ah, you tremble!

Thomas. Not from *fear*—but passion—that you——

Hansell. (*quickly*) The guilty are always fearful lest their crimes be found out.

Thomas. (*passionately*) Dare you accuse *me* of *crime?* *I*, whose tender mercy helped save you from a felon's just doom? (*draws dagger from waist and rushes at* HANSELL—NEB'S *eyes open wide with fright*) Son of a perjured mother, I'll——

Hansell. (*quickly draws revolver from hip pocket and presenting it, halts* THOMAS) You scoundrel, don't you attempt it. (*advances threatingly*) Down on your knees and swear you *lie* when you accuse *my* mother of perjury. (THOMAS *hesitates*) Down, or by the memory of my mother, I swear I'll kill you! Down! down! down! (THOMAS *drops knife, and falling to knees conceals it*) Swear it, you cowardly libel of humanity! Swear it! (*doors* L. *and* C., *are thrown open;* enter JUDGE *and* LAURA L.; DOLLY, JULIUS *and* HANS C.; NEB *standing back of sofa—all form circle with amazement depicted upon their countenances*)

Thomas. (*kneeling, with uplifted right hand*) I swear it!

QUICK DROP.

ACT II.

Scene I.—*A street in* 1 G—*time night—curtain rises to lively music.*

Enter JULIUS, L.; *general make-up dudish; crosses* R., *then returns and stands at extreme* L.; *talks as he walks.*

Julius. Well, I guess I'se done up fine 'nough to please de taste ob eben Malinda Aramintha. Dat gal am so proud an' stuck up dat she nebber steps out ob doors when de sun or moon am shinin' for fear dat she'll fall in lub wid her own shadder an' disgrace herself. (*examines himself*) Say, dese am mighty fine clothes. Dar's not anoder coon in dis town dat kin 'ford a rig like dis. I 'spect all de gals will be fussin' fur me. (*laughs*) Neb, he wanted fur to walk out wid me dis ebening, kase he knowed I 'tended to tackle de ice cream, but dis chile am 'shamed to be seen in de street wid him ; he's a common niggah! (*contemptuously*) an' can't 'ford to dress. He don't know how to raise dese fellers. (*displays a handful of silver dollars*) Dat niggah am a tryin' to play sharp on dis child all de time, but he can't pick my pocket, kase I allus totes my money in de bank. (*slaps pants pocket and puts money in right vest pocket*) He's got to get up early when he cotches me a-sleepin' wid both eyes shut! (*looks off* R.) Fo' de land sakes, who am dat a comin' ? Whew, but she am dressed scrumptious! (*tidys himself*) I 'spect she'll die right off (*laughs*) as soon as she sees dese clo's.

Enter NEB, R., *disguised as a woman ; stands* R.

Neb. (*fans himself, coyly, aside*) A culled Adonis !
Julius. (*admiringly, aside*) De Queen ob Sheba!
Neb. (*aside*) Oh, dear, I wish he would say sumfin'.
Julius. (*aside*) I'll try de 'fect ob my new rig. (*advances, raises hat and bows*) 'Scuse me for 'suming to 'dress de beauteous luminary orb dat shines so brightly afore me, but 'pears ter me dat yo'r lubly self has considered de condescentin' ob yo'r 'quaintance 'pon me afore.
Neb. (*aside*) He don't know me. (*aloud*) I wus just cognatin' wid myself whar'bouts I had de felicitous pleasure of meetin' yo', sah. May I 'quire de name ob de gem'man ?
Julius. Sartinly, miss, Julius Caesar Augustus Thomas Jefferson Crobar, *Esq.*
Neb. (*coquettishly*) Thank yo'. Well, Jule—may I call yo' Jule for short ?
Julius. Call me anything yo' like. (*aside, tickled*) She's a goner.
Neb. (*edging toward* JULIUS) Don't yo' think it am berry warm ?
Julius. (*approaching*) It am so.
Neb. (*close*) Dis wedder am so tiresome ! (*leans against* JULIUS)
Julius. (*bracing himself*) Dat am true. (*smiles*)
Neb. I wish I could rest somewhar. (*drops fan and works right hand toward* JULIUS' *vest pocket*)
Julius. (*putting right arm around* NEB) I'se at yo'r sarvice.
Neb. Oh, thank yo', yo' am so kind an' gem'manly. (*looks at* JULIUS *lovingly*)
Julius. Am yo' satisfied now ?
Neb. (*taking money from* JULIUS' *pocket*) Puffec'ly !
Julius. (*smiling*) And happy ?
Neb. Yes, wus nebber more so. (*continues removing money until* JULIUS' *pocket is empty ; places money in left hand—audience must see theft*—JULIUS *seems carried away with joy*)
Julius. Say, does anybody keep yo' reg'lar company ?
Neb. No.

Julius. Dat am good. (*doubtfully*) Maybe you don't want any, eh? (*gives* NEB *a playful squeeze*)

Neb. (*springing quickly* L., *screams—*JULIUS *sways but recovers himself*) Oh!

Julius. (*amazed*) Wot's de matter?

Neb. (*angrily*) Yo's a mean niggah to tickle me.

Julius. (*coaxingly*) Now don't git mad. I didn't mean to. Let's go and git some ice cream.

Neb. I'll hab nuffin more to do wid you ; go an' get your own ice cream. Yo's insultin', dat's wat yo' am.

Julius. I didn't mean to 'fend you. Come, an' I treat yo' to ebbery t'ing yo' wants. I'se got loads ob money, just see. (*puts hand in vest pocket ; seems puzzled ; searches trousers pocket ; looks a moment in bewilderment at* NEB *who is slowly walking* L.) Hold on dar, yo' black huzzy! Yo's picked my pocket.

Neb. (*turning angrily*) Who am yo' 'ludin' to, an' 'cusing ob stealin'?

Julius. (*excitedly*) Yo'! Gib me my money, or I'll call de perlice, and hab yo' 'rested.

Neb. Gib yo' back what money?

Julius. De money you stole frum me.

Neb. (*advances and speaks significantly*) Stole frum you?

Julius. Yes, took frum my pocket.

Neb. Look heah, Mr. Niggah, do yo' know who yo's a talkin' to?

Julius. Yes, I do, and if yo' don't hand ober dat money, I'll bust your old cocoanut fur yo'. (*holds cane aloft*)

Neb. (*threateningly*) Yo' will, will yo'? Take that! (*strikes* JULIUS *and knocks him down—quickly removing hat and wig, he changes silver dollars from left to right hand, one at a time, exclaiming*) Julius Caesar Augustus Thomas Jefferson Crobar, *Esq.*, (*shakes money at him*) Good ebening. I'll buy my own ice cream. (*gathering dress in hand, runs off* R.—JULIUS *springs to feet, picks up hat and cane quickly, talking*)

Julius. De blamed black niggah, he'll nebber fool me ag'in. I hope dat ice cream will choke him ; if it don't, *I will*, sartin' and sure. (*run off*, R.)

Enter OFFICER *with* HANSELL, *handcuffed*, L.; *at same instant* enter THOMAS R.—*as they pass, a look of mutual hatred passes between* HANSELL *and* THOMAS—*as* THOMAS *reaches* L., *he stops and whistles softly—*OFFICER *and* HANSELL *turn—*THOMAS *approaches, calls* OFFICER *aside.*

Thomas. (*places coin in* OFFICER'S *hand*) I would like to have a few moment's private conversation with that man. (*pointing to*

Hansell) Will you step aside and leave us alone for five minutes?

Officer. (*looking at coin ; hesitates*) I—don't know—that—I can trust you——

Thomas. (*handing him another coin*) Perhaps that will help you decide.

Officer. (*examing coin*) Think of my responsibility, were he to escape——

Thomas. No danger of that, I assure you. You know *me* too well to suppose *I* would lend him assistance to effect that. However, if you have any fears for the safety of your prisoner, or apprehension in regard to yourself—this (*adding another coin*) will no doubt dispel them.

Officer. (*bowing*) Thank you, I will step aside, but, mark me, (*smiles*) I shall keep a strict watch upon you both. (*crosses to* Hansell) Remain here a moment while I speak to Coons over there. (*points toward and* exits R.)

Thomas. (*crosses to* Hansell) I am sorry, Hansell, to see you publicly disgraced.

Hansell. Your *sympathy* is not desired, and it is as *insulting* as it is *uncalled for.*

Thomas. Believe me, Hansell, your arrest was not made at my instigation. *My* wishes were not consulted The Judge, whose guest I was, took the whole matter into his own hands, and made *my* quarrel, *his own.*

Hansell. Quite likely !

Thomas. You doubt me ?

Hansell. I do, and *ever shall!*

Thomas. You speak bitterly ; yet I bear you no malice, and shall even yet try to aid you. I presume you are on your way to the magistrate's office for a hearing ?

Hansell. I am.

Thomas. As the evidence now stands, what do you expect ?

Hansell. The full penalty of the law.

Thomas. Suppose a way were to be opened up whereby you could be acquitted of the charge preferred against you, what would you do?

Hansell. That would depend upon circumstances, and to *whom* I would be indebted.

Thomas. Suppose I were to perform that act of kindness.

Hansell. (*quickly*) You?

Thomas. Yes, *I.*

Hansell. How ?

Thomas. Listen. The Judge and his household were witnesses of your deadly assault upon me, yet *they* know absolutely nothing of what provoked it. Suppose, on the witness stand, I deny what you will allege, that you acted in self-defense, what proof have you to sustain you?

Hansell. The *knife* you dropped when thwarted by me!

Thomas. No one saw that knife but yourself. When I fell, the skirt of my coat concealed it, and when I rose that tell-tale evidence was missing.

Hansell. Then indeed is my case hopeless!

Thomas. Just so, unless I aid you. Suppose I sustain your evidence by acknowledging *I* was the aggressive party——

Hansell. Well?

Thomas. What will you do?

Hansell. Thank you for being *honest* enough once in your life to tell the *truth!*

Thomas. Be careful, Hansell, and remember you are in my power.

Hansell. I realize my position thoroughly. Upon what conditions do you propose to *tell the truth ?*

Thomas. That you cease your attentions to Miss Bell, and use your influence with her in *my* behalf.

Hansell. Then I am to purchase my liberty at the expense of my heart's sufferings?

Thomas. If you so consider it, yes.

Hansell. (*sneeringly*) Your *kindness* is indeed affecting!

Thomas. I cannot help it, it's my nature, you know.

Hansell. Well, sir——

Thomas. (*interrupting*) Before you decide, weigh well your answer.

Hansell. I have.

Thomas. Think of your mother and sister.

Hansell. They are ever present in my thoughts.

Thomas. The privations and sufferings they must endure if the means of their support is cut off by your imprisonment——

Hansell. I have.

Thomas. And your answer?

Hansell. Were I relieved of these irons, I would throttle you until your lying, deceitful tongue were stilled in the embrace of death.

Thomas. (*advancing in a passion, with uplifted fist*) You insulting, ungrateful cur, I'll——

Hansell. *Strike!* Now your true nature is asserting itself. (*speaks vehemently*) Sooner than obtain freedom on your conditions and be under obligations to *you*, I would see my loved ones consigned to pauperism, and *myself* in the toils of starvation.

Thomas. (*passionately*) Go to your doom then. I am done with you.

Re-enter OFFICER, R.

Officer. (*taking* HANSELL *by arm*) Come, time's up.

Exeunt, R.

Thomas. (*following*) Lead on! I follow to *seal* his fate.

Exit, R.—*scene changes to*

Scene II.—*Home of* MRS. HANSELL—*table* R. 2 E. *with lighted lamp, pitcher of water, glass and open old family Bible on it*— MRS. HANSELL *seated at table*—MARY *lying on couch—soft music.*

Mrs. H. (*closing Bible*) I wish this cruel suspense were over and I knew what to expect. That Henry would attempt to take a fellow-being's life in other than self-defense, I cannot believe. The magistrate *must* believe what Henry says is true, even if the evidence of others contradicts his. If I were only permitted to be present at his hearing, to encourage him and let him know that there was at least *one* near him who believed what he said! But, vain regret! How long, oh, how long must the shadow continue to mock the substance! Would it not be better to throw off the mask and reveal——

Mary. (*interrupting*) Mrs. Hansell.

Mrs. H. (*rises, and approaches bed*) What is it, darling?

Mary. Please give me a drink.

Mrs. H. (*going to table*) Certainly, my dear. (*fills glass and returns to bed; raises* MARY *with right arm, and gives her water*) Are you feeling better, now?

Mary. Yes, ma'am, thank you.

Mrs. H. You must try to go to sleep again.

Mary. Where is papa?

Mrs. H. He went out a few moments ago.

Mary. Will he be in again soon?

Mrs. H. I hope so, dear.

Mary. (*half rises, leans on elbow*) I wish he were here. I had such a horrid dream about him, I thought he was with a lot of bad men who were setting fire to houses and burning them up. Oh, dear, I wish he were here!

Mrs. H. Don't worry, Mary; lie down and go to sleep, and perhaps your next dream will be a pleasant one. (MARY *resumes former position*) Papa will soon be in again, I hope. (*goes to table*) I, too, wish he were here. Henry feared this morning that night would usher in a reign of arson and terror. The mill hands have become desperate and beyond control, but I hope and pray no violence may be done to man or property. (*knock at door*) Come in.

Enter LAURA *hastily; she glances—back at door and seems startled —goes to* MRS. HANSELL'S *side—music stops.*

Laura. May I remain here a few moments, Mrs. Hansell? (*appears nervous*)

Mrs. H. (*rising*) Certainly, my child. Why, what has alarmed you?

Laura. I was being followed by some vicious looking men, who appeared bereft of reason.

Mrs. H. (*astonished*) " Followed by men who seemed bereft of reason!" Why, Laura, what do you mean!

Laura. Just what I said. They hooted at me, taunted me about my " fine clothing," " jaunty airs," and " proud carriage," and said that before the sun rose to-morrow *I* would know what it was to be homeless.

Mrs. H. What caused them to follow you?

Laura. I know not. They were standing on the corner, and as I passed through their midst some one called out " There goes the Judge's treasure," and then they all laughed. After I had gone a few steps I noticed that they were following me. As I quickened my pace so did they, keeping up a running exchange of the most brutal expressions I ever heard. Seeking to escape them, I thought of you and hastened here, knowing you would shelter me until all danger was past.

Mrs. H. Certainly I will.

Laura. I never knew we had so many vicious looking men in our town as I saw on the streets to-night. The corners were lined with them and all seemed to be laboring under the most intense excitement. I fear there is trouble ahead for some one.

Mrs. H. (*aside*) And *I* fear so, too. (*aloud*) What were you doing in the street at this hour, unattended?

Laura. I was just returning from your son's examination. I was summoned as a witness. You know I saw the (*contemptuously*) *assault.*

Mrs. H. (*anxiously*) Yes, but you don't really think Henry intended to kill Mr. Thomas, do you?

Laura. (*with spirit*) I cannot say, but if *he did*, I *know* he would have *just cause* for the act.

Mrs. H. (*eagerly*) Why?

Laura. (*quickly*) Because he is too *noble*—too good—to be guilty of—(*embarrassed*) Oh, Mrs. Hansell, please excuse me, I did not mean to—Oh, what have I done?

Mrs. H. (*quickly*) Filled *my* heart with joy unspeakable to know that there is *another* who considers *my* son incapable of being influenced by the *motives* that govern the average man's action.

Laura. (*sees bed*) Oh, Mrs. Hansell, whom have you there? (*pointing to bed*)

Mrs. H. Joe Harris's child. Poor Joe was turned out of his house to-day, because he was unable to pay his rent, and he sought temporary shelter here for his sick child. These are terrible times for the poor, Miss Laura. No work and no near prospect of any!

Laura. I know it. I do wish the Judge would re-open his mill. I have pleaded with him again and again, but all to no purpose.

Mrs. H. I fear if he does not soon relent he will regret his action, for Henry told me—(*abruptly, with earnestness*) Oh, Miss Laura, tell me, do you think there is a possibility of Henry's being able to clear himself of the charges preferred against him?

Laura. I—(*hesitates*)

Mrs. H. (*grasping her by arm*) Tell me the truth!

Laura. (*sadly*) No, I fear not, for the testimony of Mr. Thomas, the Judge, our servants and *my own* was all against him. I did not wait to hear what his plea was, but left as soon as I was released from duty. (MRS. HANSELL *seems distressed*) But no matter, Mrs. Hansell, what occurs, you need have no uneasiness as to *your* future, for as long as I have a dollar in this world to call my own, it shall be shared with you.

Mrs. H. Noble girl! I thank you for this proof of your love and generosity, but it was not of *myself* I was thinking, it was Henry's sufferings.

Laura. Let us hope for the best, trust in "Him who never forsakes," and do our duty. May I inquire why you were not present this evening to cheer and comfort your son? I was somewhat surprised at your absence.

Mrs. H. (*distressed*) I cannot tell you. My only excuse must be my aversion to appearing in public.

Laura. Pardon me, if I distress you, but may I inquire why you are so closely veiled whenever you appear on the street?

Mrs. H. (*appears agitated*) No, no, my child, you must not ask; it is a mere whim—a fancy of mine contracted long, long ago, which still clings to me. Ask not the grave to give up its dead! Ah, but it does, of its own free will, too! Its hideous spectral forms, unmasked, stalk forth, chilling the sunbeams and blasting life's sweetest blessings. How much longer must I bear this torture? (LAURA *approaches and lays her hand upon* MRS. HANSELL'S *shoulder*)

Laura. (*soothingly*) There, there, Mrs. Hansell, I am sorry my rudeness awakened unpleasant memories; let—(*the door is opened quickly and* NEB *bounds in, unnoticed by* MRS. HANSELL *and* LAURA)

Neb. (*swinging hat and manifesting great joy*) Hurrah! (MRS. HANSELL *and* LAURA *scream*—MARY, *startled, rises on left elbow*) Hurrah! hurrah! hurrah! (*twirls round on heel and seems demented*)

Laura. (*commandingly*) What do you mean, Neb, by entering here so abruptly, and yelling as though you were crazy? See—(*points to* MARY) You have roused that poor sick child from her slumbers and frightened her terribly.

Neb. (*joyously*) I can't help it, Miss Laura. By golly, if I don't holler, I'll bust. I'se feel so happy an' good, dat I could jine meeting widout any preparation whatsumeber. (*goes to bed abruptly*) Say, little one, yo' must 'scuse me if I skeered yo', kase I didn't mean to. I didn't know you wus sick. (*with energy*) Yo' must hurry up an' git well, an' I'll buy you lots ob t'ings, see if I don't. (*throws hat on floor and kicks it up stage*) Whoop! I 'spects, Miss Laura, yo'd better be a gwine home, fur de Judge wus all fired mad when he found you had left afore him. (*goes to hat, takes it on toe of shoe, tosses it up and catches it, laughing to himself*)

Laura. What is the matter with you, Neb, are you crazy?

Neb. (*grinning*) Really, Miss Laura, I dunno; 'spects I is, or nigh about dat. De fact is—(*suddenly to* Mrs. Hansell) I 'clar to goodness, I forgot to tell yo', mum, what I ran all de way here fur. Massa Henry am cl'ared, gone free!

Mrs. H. (*sinking to chair*) Thank Heaven!

Laura. (*eagerly at* Mrs. Hansell's L. *side ;* Neb, L. 2 E.) Who told you?

Neb. Nobody told me. *I* sot him free!

Laura. (*amazed*) You set him free?

Neb. Dat am a fact, sure.

Laura. How?

Neb. By my ev'dence 'roberating de testimony ob de pris'ner. Dat's wat de mag'strate said.

Laura. *Your evidence!* Why, what did you know about the case? You were not in the house when the trouble occurred. I had sent you for some lemons.

Neb. 'Sidering de sarvice I'se rendered justice, I hope, Miss Laura, yo'll 'scuse me, but I forgot all 'bout dem lemons.

Laura. Then you *were* in the house, after all?

Neb. Yes, mum, my ev'dence proved dat fo' sure.

Laura. Where?

Neb. In de 'ception-room.

Laura. (*looking at him searchingly*) Neb!

Neb. Mum.

Laura. Are you telling the truth?

Neb. (*rolling his eyes*) I 'clare, Miss Laura, yo'r 'spicions am unjust.

Laura. I am sorry, Neb, that circumstances justify them. I did not see *you* in the reception-room when I entered it, nor while I remained there. I cannot believe you were present.

Neb. But I wus, tho', all de same.

Laura. Where were you then?

Neb. Behind de sofa.

Laura. (*surprised*) Behind the sofa!

Neb. Yes, mum.

Laura. What were you doing there?

Neb. Layin' low for dat black Julius, an' if I had kotched him 'bout dat time, he'd seed shootin' stars for sartin. Yo' see he—

Laura. (*interrupting*) Yes, yes, you can tell me another time what he did. I want to know——

Neb. (*interrupting*) Yo' wants to know what I seed? Well, I'll tell yo'. (*talks rapidly*) Arter de Judge an' Massa Henry done been talking a while dey got to sassin' one anoder. Massa Henry was spunky, an' de way he sassed de Judge 'twas wond'ful. Soon de Judge he got mad an' ordered Massa Henry out de house. I jest wish you could a seed de Judge; he swelled out 'till he most filled de room. (*laughs*) By golly, I 'spected ebbery minnit to see him bust! Den in comes Mr. Thomas; an' de Judge an' him talks a few minnits 'bout you—(*abruptly*) Say, do yo' know dat feller 'tends to lub yo', but (*chuckles*) I 'spects he'd better switch off ob de main line an' lay ober, for when de bull-gine comes a thunderin' along wid Massa Henry as de eng'neer, I 'spects to see yo' step aboard his train, eh?

Laura. (*quickly interrupting and looking anxiously at* MRS. HANSELL) Hush! hush!

Neb. (*resuming narrative*) Soon de Judge leaves de room to call yo', when back comes Massa Henry. He an' old Thomas flare up as soon as dey seed one anoder, like two fightin' roosters. Massa Henry was slow to come to time, so Mr. Thomas got in de fust lick—a slappin' blow on Massa Henry's cheek—an' called him a coward an' a lot ob sich mean names. I 'spected ebbery minnit to see Massa Henry rise right up an' wipe up de floor wid him; but he didn't, he kept cool an' made 'rangements right dar to fit Mr. Thomas in a few days wid shot guns, pistols an' knives. I'se gwine to be on hand when dat comes off!

Mrs. H. (*alarmed*) You do not mean there is to be a duel between them, do you?

Neb. I dunno, but I guess dat's what dey meant. Arter de 'rangements, dey took breff, den dey began callin' each odder names *right*. Mr. Thomas started fur Massa Henry ag'in, but he wus ready fur him dis time, so Thomas he skeered. Den he commenced callin' yo', (*to* MRS. HANSELL) mum, names. Den yo'—(*enthusiastically*) ought to seed Massa Henry. He rose taller'n de stove pipe, his eyes spread out like saucers, an' looked like two red hot furnaces, his fists swelled up till dey wus as big as mountains. Thomas wus no whar, so he pulls out a knife so long (*extends hands apart, suiting action to each word*) rushes at Massa Henry who draws a shootin' iron, an' made Mr. Thomas swear dat what he said 'bout yo', mum, (*to* MRS. HANSELL) wus a lie. (*rubbing hands*) Jiminy crickitees! it wus better'n a play. (*tosses hat in air and laughs to himself*)

Laura. So, then, your testimony *proved* Mr. Hansell's plea of self-defense?

Enter HANSELL, *unperceived, except by* NEB; *approaches softly toward* MRS. HANSELL, *shaking finger warningly at* NEB.

Neb. (*seems tickled*) Dat's it, exactly.

Mrs. H. Where is Henry?

Hansell. (*at back of chair*) Here, mother. (*lays hand on her shoulder*) Sit still, do not rise, please. (*bows to* LAURA) Excuse me, Miss Bell, for presuming to advise you, but the *sooner* you reach your home, the less will be the danger you run of being seen on the streets. Neb, there, who has proved himself a *friend* to me, will afford you ample protection.

Mrs. H. Henry, don't you think *you* had better accompany Miss Bell? She was compelled to seek shelter here but a short time ago, to escape a crowd of men who were following her.

Hansell. I cannot. It is impossible. My services are needed elsewhere this very moment. There is not a possibility of Miss Bell's meeting any one between here and her residence, provided she leaves at once. (*speaks rapidly*)

Laura. I will follow your advice. Good-night, Mrs. Hansell, I thank you for your kindness. Come, Neb. (*starts for door preceded by* HANSELL *who holds it open, and bows as* LAURA *and* NEB *pass out; closes door and goes down* C. *quickly*)

Mrs. H. Henry, need I say how rejoiced I am to see you free and——

Hansell. (*interrupting*) Excuse me, mother, I well know how thankful *you* feel at my release, and your joy finds a response within *my* heart, that I am enabled once more to help support and sustain you; but *talking* just now is out of the question, for I must away. (*starts for door, but stops as* MRS. HANSELL *speaks*)

Mrs. H. (*surprised*) Where?

Hansell. Excuse me, again, mother——

Mrs. H. (*alarmed*) Henry, you are not going to——

Hansell. (*quickly*) Pardon me, dear mother, but I would rather not tell you. I should not have come directly home after my release, had I known Neb had informed you of it, but attended first to the business I now seek to transact.

Mrs. H. (*leaving table and coming to* HENRY'S R. *side*) Henry!

Hansell. (*beseechingly*) Please, mother, do not attempt to detain me. What I can do must be done quickly. I will soon return.

Mrs. H. (*significantly*) Yes, but will it be *dead* or *alive?*

Hansell. (*surprised*) Why, what do you mean?

Mrs. H. (*slowly, walking backward toward door—*HANSELL *turns so as to face her*) I know of your contemplated duel with Mr. Thomas.

Hansell. (*starts*) Who told you?

Mrs. H. (*keeps her eyes fastened upon him*) Neb!

Hansell. (*quickly*) But my going out has no reference to that.

Mrs. H. (*at door*) We shall see.

Hansell. Mother, do you doubt me?

Mrs. H. For the first time in my life I am *compelled* to say *I do.*

Hansell. (*quickly*) Then *doubt* me no longer, for I will tell you my mission. There is to be an attempt made to burn the Judge's mill, and I fear, his residence, too, to-night. Knowing my influence with the men, I intend using it to get them to abandon their rash project if possible.

Mrs. H. (*significantly*) Was it not the Judge who had you arrested?

Hansell. (*quickly*) I believe it was.

Mrs. H. And was it not the *Judge* who caused our *neighbors* and *ourselves* to suffer the pangs of hunger during the past six months?

Hansell. Partly so.

Mrs. H. Is he not responsible for the desperate straits in which the poor of our town find themselves?

Hansell. To a certain extent, yes.

Mrs. H. Is he your friend?

Hansell. No!

Mrs. H. Is he mine?

Hansell. No!

Mrs. H. Is he your fellow workmen's?

Hansell. No!

Mrs. H. And yet you seek to do him a kindness?

Hansell. I do.

Mrs. H. Knowing him to be a bitter foe of your mother's, an enemy of your neighbors', and a purse-proud unfeeling aristocrat?

Hansell. I cannot help that.

Mrs. H. Have you no desire to revenge his cruelty to you?

Hansell. Not at the expense of his property.

Mrs. H. Nor resent the injury done *your own mother?*

Hansell. Not by the torch.

Mrs. H. Not even if *your mother* were to plead with you upon her bended knees?

Hansell. Never! There is a law and love above even the sanctity of a mother's, and he who transgresses it by applying the torch of malice to a fellow-being's property, disgraces the mother who bore him, and covers with infamy the heritage left him by his father!

Mrs. H. Henry!

Hansell. Listen, mother. As a loyal man, my duty is to preserve the Judge's property from destruction, if it be in my power; and *that duty I will perform,* even though it cost me all I possess, including my mother's cherished love.

Mrs. H. Thank Heaven! you are above yielding to the petty passions that warp and sway the actions of your sex. This is the proudest moment of my life. In carrying out your purpose you fulfil *my* wishes and prove to the world the nobility of your character.

Hansell. (*starts for door*) There, mother, that will do.

Mrs. H. Stop one moment, please. Before you leave this room you must promise me to give up your contemplated duel with Mr. Thomas.

Hansell. I cannot. My word of honor is pledged to resent his insult.

Mrs. H. (*barring door with body*) *Then* you cannot leave—except by *force.*

Hansell. But, mother——

Mrs. H. Entreaties are vain, arguments useless! The field of so-called "*honor*" is one of *disgrace*, and no *true* man would ever seek to avenge a *fancied* or a *real* injury at the price of a human soul.

Hansell. You do not understand.

Mrs. H. I understand enough to know that if you carry out your intention you will transgress a commandment of your Maker's and break your mother's heart.

Hansell. Sooner than do *that* I will submit to any shame, bear all the taunting jeers of my companions bravely, and be *happy* amid them, knowing that my action has brought peace and happiness to you.

Mrs. H. Nobly spoken! (*throws door open, steps R. of it and points with left hand out of open door*) Go, and may Heaven's blessing attend you and crown your mission with success. (HANSELL *quickly* exits ; *scene closed in*)

Scene III.—*A street in first grooves.*

Enter THOMAS, R.; *comes* C.

Thomas. The miscarriage of justice, occasioned by the shrewdness of that infernal Neb, has again given Hansell a chance to win Laura. That was a blundering piece of work of mine and will cost me the Judge's friendship. How to regain it, is what is now troubling me. (*thinks*) Ah, I have an idea!—that's capital! What is to prevent me from disguising myself as a mechanic, joining the horde that intend burning the Judge's mill and residence, rescuing Laura, becoming a hero, and eventually, out of gratitude, Laura's husband? Nothing! I'll do it. (*starts for* L.—enter JULIUS L., *passes to* R. *of* THOMAS)

Julius. (*raises hat*) Good eben', Massa Thomas.

Thomas. (L.) Anything new?

Julius. No, sah, 'ceptin' de Judge am all fired mad at yo' for trying dat knife bis'ness.

Thomas. You must think I'm a fool not to be aware of that!

Julius. (*raises hat*) T'ank yo', sah.

Thomas. For what?

Julius. For telling me yo' am *not* a fool.

Thomas. (*starts for* JULIUS) You impertinent black——

Julius. (*pulling off hat and starting to run*) It am no use, yo' can't kotch me. (THOMAS *stops* L. C., *and retraces his steps* L.; JULIUS *comes* R. C.) Say, Massa Thomas. (THOMAS *stops and turns*) Yo' forgot sumfin'! (*slaps pocket*)

Thomas. (*takes coin from pocket and tosses it at* JULIUS' *feet*) There, you dog, take it. It will be the last you get from me for some time.   Exit L.

Julius. (*picking up coin*) Dat's what he allus says, but I guess I kin fotch him again, when I'se ready. (*examines coin*) Whew; five dollars! I must make two more to get even with what Neb stole.   Exit R.

Enter HANS, R., *walking backward with both hands grasping handles of covered market basket,* JULIUS *following, trying to pull basket from him.*

Hans. Dot vos a lie. I didn't steal nodings.

Julius. You did. Whar did yo' git dis basket?

Hans. Dot be mine peesness.

Julius. Yo' stole it. Now, if yo' don't hand me over two dollars at once, I'll hab yo' 'rested by de fust perlice I meets.

Enter NEB, L., *disguised as policeman—wears moustache and side whiskers, helmet over his own hat; breast padded with coffee sack; carries stuffed billy in right hand—slowly approaches back of* HANS.

Hans. I tells you dot I steals nodings, und I kin shust lick enny purleece dot efer drew breff.

Julius. (*sees policeman, lets go of basket*) Oh, Lor'! Oh, Lor'! (*pulls off hat and runs out* R.—*at same instant* NEB, *who has reached* HANS, *strikes him on back of head with billy*)

Hans. (*alarmed*) Mein Gott, vot vos dot?

Neb. (*changes voice*) What's that?

Hans. (*turns, drops basket, and seems terribly frightened*) Meester purleece, I vos shust foolin' mit dot poy.

Neb. I can't help that. Yo' are my pris'ner now; (*lays right hand on* HANS' *shoulder*) an' must go wid me.

Hans. Vere to?

Neb. To de station house.

Hans. (*affrighted*) An' schleep mit de rats und mice all grawlin' over me?

Neb. Dat's whar yo'll hab to sleep to-night, an' it will cost yo' four dollars an' fifty cents to get out in de mawnin'.

Hans. Mein Gott, dot will broke me! Let me see; (*takes money from right trousers pocket and counts it*) ein, zwei, drei, vier, und ein halber thaler.

Neb. (*slightly advances*) It will cost yo' four dollars and a half to *git* out in de morning, and it will cost yo' four dollars an' fifty cents to *keep* out to-night. (*looks ahead of him*)

Hans. (*not comprehending*) Vot ish dot?

Neb. (*impatiently*) Fork ober, an' (*pointing with left hand,* L.) git! (HANS *places money in* NEB'S *right hand, picks up basket, walks slowly* L. *glancing uneasily at* NEB, *till near wing, then rushes out* L.—NEB *examines money eagerly*) Haul No. 2! (*looks off* R.; *startled, resumes original tone of voice*) By Jupiter, if dar ain't a reg'lar cop a comin' dis way! (*quickly pulls off helmet and coat, picks up coffee sack, hastily puts coat, helmet and billy in it, rolls it up and tucks it under left arm*) Seven from Julius, four fifty from Hans—eleven dollars an' fifty cents. My new suit am all right! (*starts* R. *singing softly,* "*In de morning by de bright light.*"

Exit R., *scene changes.*

Scene IV.—*The exterior of* JUDGE BUTTONS' *house*—enter *mob,* L., *with axes, ropes and lanterns, led by* THOMAS, *disguised; range along* L. *wings and up* L.—THOMAS *up* L.

Thomas. (*aside*) Now, for my last bold move, and then for Laura, opulence and ease! (*aloud to men*) Boys, yonder stands (*pointing to house*) the palatial residence of our common foe—the king of monopolists! Shall it remain standing as a gigantic hydra, menacing the liberties of our children, or shall it return to the dust from which it sprang?

Mob. (*in unison*) Fire it, burn it to the ground! (*enter two men* L., *carrying bags filled with shavings—at same instant enter* HAN-SELL L., *with coat and hat off; he pushes men aside and ascends steps* R.)

Hansell. Men, brothers, fellow-workmen, in Heaven's name, desist! Think of what you are doing! Already the Judge's mill lies in ashes. Are you not satisfied? Is not your vengeance appeased? For the love of your mothers, wives and little ones, add not this crime to the many already laid at the door of Labor.

Thomas. (*to men*) Remove him! (*two men spring to obey; they seize* HANSELL *and force him out* R. *as* THOMAS *speaks*) He is *no friend of ours.* He is a *traitor.* Pile up the fagots, (*men place bags against house, bring on coal oil barrel with conflagration pot inside, place it near bags and ignite fire in pot,* THOMAS *talking all* *the time*) and let the heavens above us reëcho Labor's cheers as the despot's wealth ascends in smoke and flame.

Re-enter HANSELL, R., *followed by* HANS *and* NEB ; *seizing barrel, they start for* C. *when mob makes a rush for them—simultaneously door is opened and* LAURA, *dressed in pure white, appears with revolver in hand, followed by* JULIUS *with blunderbuss.*

Laura. (L. *on steps, presenting revolver*) Back, every man of you ! The first one who steps forward is a dead man ! (*mob falls back,* L.)

Julius. (R., *on steps, covering men*) Yes, an' de next dozen and a half ob yo's. (*descends steps as* HANSELL, HANS *and* NEB, *place barrel* C.) Come on, yo's a bully set of fellers, I'se ready for yo' !

Neb. (*back of barrel, swinging hat and cheering lustily*) De Judge's home am safe ! Hurrah ! hurrah ! hurrah !

MOB. L. *and up* L., *huddled together crestfallen—*THOMAS *up* L., *trying to pull hat over eyes—*LAURA *on steps with revolver directed at men—*HANS *on her* R.—HANSELL L., *with gaze riveted upon* THOMAS—JULIUS *up* R., *with gun at shoulder, covering men—* NEB C., *back of barrel, waving hat and cheering.*

PICTURE.

SLOW DROP.

ACT III.

Scene.—*Same as Act I—as curtain rises* DOLLY *is wiping organ with cloth—*JULIUS *dusting sofa with brush—curtain rises to lively music.*

Dolly. I don't believe it !

Julius. Well, I jest guess I heerd de Jedge say so.

Dolly. When ?

Julius. Las' night, arter de mob left.

Dolly. Where ?

Julius. In dis berry room.

Dolly. To whom was he talking ?

Julius. To *me.*

Dolly. To you ! (*laughs*) That's a likely story. Do you expect me to believe it ?

Julius. Blamed if I care wedder you do or no. (*brushes vigorously*)

Dolly. The idea of the Judge making a confidant of you! (*laughs*) It's too absurd for anything.

Julius. (*pausing in work*) Look a heah, Dolly——

Dolly. (*sharply, interrupting*) Whom are you addressing?

Julius. (*quickly*) *Miss* Dolly, den. (*aside*) Darn her rubbers! (*aloud*) I 'spose yo' t'inks de Jedge nebber confides in me; but he does, all de same. Of'en an' of'en he's told me heaps of t'ings dat he wouldn't t'ink ob tellin' (*contemptuously*) de rest ob de sarvents.

Dolly. I don't believe the Judge ever told you he intended rebuilding his mill.

Julius. Yo' don't, eh? (*with importance*) I guess dat wusn't all de Jedge told me e'der.

Dolly. It wasn't?

Julius. No, it wusn't.

Dolly. What else did he tell you?

Julius. I won't tell yo', it am none ob your bis'nes.

Dolly. (*laughs in an irritating manner*) Oh, no; of *course* you won't tell me!

Julius. (*irritated*) No, I won't.

Dolly. (*irritatingly*) Certainly not, that's right! I wouldn't if I were you, either. When persons *pretend* to know something of importance, they always act just as you are doing.

Julius. But I *knows* wot I'se talkin' 'bout—I——

Dolly. (*interrupting*) No, you don't!

Julius. (*exasperated*) I don't, eh?

Dolly. No!

Julius. Why doesn't I?

Dolly. Because you would not allow me to doubt your word if you did.

Julius. Yo' won't believe me if I tells yo'——

Dolly. Try me and see.

Julius. Well den—(*hesitates*) No, I won't e'der! Yo'll jest poke fun at me ag'in.

Dolly. (*contemptuously*) Now, I'm sure you are only *pretending* to know something, or you wouldn't be *afraid* of being laughed at; you are a *coward!*

Julius. Who's a coward?

Dolly. You are.

Julius. (*excited*) Does yo' knows who yo's a talkin' to?

Dolly. (*coolly*) Certainly I do.

Julius. (*taking a step forward*) Yo's had better be keerful——

Dolly. (*going quickly to* C.) What's that? Do you know whom *you* are talking to?

Julius. (*quickly subsiding*) I—mean—dat yo' might hab sum 'sideration fur a fellah's feelin's. (*resumes dusting in a jerky, angry manner, muttering to himself*)

Dolly. It is well for you that you cooled down and changed the tone of your voice, for in another momènt, I would have made you *feel* who it was *you* were addressing in that insolent manner. (*turning* R., *she glances over* L, *shoulder, then smiles to herself—resumes work*)

Julius. (*doggedly*) I'se no bigger coward dan yo' is.

Dolly. Then why don't you tell what you are aching to. (JULIUS *mutters to himself*) Oh, you needn't talk to yourself and try to assume a mysterious air to mislead me. You know nothing of the Judge's future intentions. You can't fool me.

Julius. Nobody is a tryin' to fool yo'.

Dolly. No, not *now*, but you *were* a moment ago.

Julius. No, I wusn't e'der, fur I knows sumfin' dat would make yo'r eyes fly open so wide, dat it would take dem free weeks to git shut agin.

Dolly. (*comes* C., *claps hands*) Oh, tell me, please, what is it?

Julius. 'Pears ter me dat you am a *achin'* wusser to hear wot I knows, dan I is to tell it!

Dolly. Out with it, or you are a *coward!*

Julius. (*comes* L. *of* DOLLY) Well, de Jedge, says, says he, Julius——

Dolly. (*eagerly*) Yes, yes, but go on——

Julius. I 'tend to——

Enter HANS C. D., *coatless, has shirt-sleeves rolled up, large white apron on, marks of flour on face and arms, paper cap on head; stands* C.

Hans. (*speaks excitedly*) Say, Mees Dolly, how do you vant dot durkey stuffed?

Dolly. Why, the usual way, Hans.

Hans. You no vant lemon juice mixed mit it?

Dolly. Why, no.

Hans. Nein, nor garlic?

Dolly. Certainly not!

Hans. Nor orange peelin's, nor apples, und sheese——

Dolly. Of course not. Don't you know how to make filling for fowls?

Hans. Yah, I knows, but dot Jule, dar, tole me dot you vanted dem dings in, too.

Julius. (*quickly*) I nebber said ennyt'ing ob de kind. I jest axes him if eber he *tried* dat receipt.

Hans. (*angrily*) You youst did say so——

Julius. (*angrily*) I didn't. Now look a'heah, Dutchy, if yo' tells enny more lies on me, I'll make yo' prove dem afore a mad'-strate. I'se gittin' tired ob habin' my chac'ter fur 'racity 'sailed by de likes ob yo'.

Hans. (*angrily, advancing upon* JULIUS) Who tells dem lies?

Julius. (*retreating down* L.) Keep away from me, or yo'll git hurt!

Dolly. (*authoritatively*) Stop your quarrelling this instant, both of you! Hans, return to your duties in the kitchen.

Hans. (*shaking fist at* JULIUS) Youst you come ouf in meine kitchen. I youst bounds you up mit mein fists till you looks like ein sausage meat! (*going*) Come ouf, come ouf! **Exit** C. D.

Dolly. (C., *speaks pleasantly*) Now, Julius, I'm ready to hear your story. Don't waste any time or some one may come in and interrupt you again.

Julius. If I tells yo', yo'll let dat turkey stuffin' bis'nes pass, won't yo'?

Dolly. Yes, yes.

Julius. Kase yo' see, I didn't mean nuffin' by it. Dat Dutchman b'lieves ennyt'ing dat yo' tells him.

Dolly. (*figgetty*) Yes, yes, I know all that—go on with your story!

Julius. (*aside*) She's gettin' de figgits! Wimmin folks has de mostest cur'osity ob enny an'mal dat breeves. (*aloud*) De Jedge tole me dat on 'count ob de sarvice we did him las' night, dat he 'tended to 'crease mine, an' Neb's, an' Hans' wages a dollar a week, an' make us a present besides, and dat he 'tended to build up his mill ag'in an' make dat Mr. Hansell de superintendent ob it.

Dolly. (*joyously*) Did he *really* and *truly* tell you that?

Julius. (*tickled*) As suah as yo' am a libin', he did.

Dolly. Do you think he was in earnest?

Julius. He wus dat. Yo' oughter seed him a walkin' up an' down dis room; he wus a-cryin' one minnit, an' cussin' de next; swearin' dat me, Neb an' Hans wus sum 'count arter all. Oh, he wus all worked up, an' I 'spected ebbery minnit dat he'd hab a fit of night sweats or sumfin' else.

Dolly. (*joyously*) Oh, I'm so glad! If Henry—I mean Mr. Hansell—should get that position it would be just delightful!

Julius. 'Pears dat yo' am mighty int'rested in dat Mr. Hansell.

Dolly. So I am!

Julius. (*grinning*) Oh, I see; yo' am kinder gone on him, but yo' needn't be skeered, I'll not tell on yo'!

Dolly. There's nothing *to tell*. Mr. Hansell is my——(*aside*) I came near letting out my secret! (*aloud*) Now go on with your work. (DOLLY *goes to melodeon and* JULIUS *to sofa; both resume work*—DOLLY *with back to* L. D. *talking*) For my part. I don't believe the Judge—(**enter** JUDGE L. D. *quietly; he stands near table* L., *looking at* DOLLY, *while rapid transitions of feeling play upon his features*—JULIUS *notices him the instant he enters, seems startled, casts a quick glance at* DOLLY *and quietly sneaks out of* C. D.,

but immediately reappears; peeps in and enjoys the scene—as
DOLLY *screams he springs up as though affrighted*)—will carry
out the promises he made last night. You can't place any depend-
ence on anything he says. One moment he'll say he'll do this,
and the next do the opposite. In the *morning* he'll be pleasant, in
the *afternoon* cross, snappish and surly, and in the *evening* he'll be
storming around and almost take your head off if you look at him.
He's a nasty, ill-tempered old thing, more like a *brute* than a man.
I just wish I had the handling of him for a year or two, I'd——

Judge. Dolly !

Dolly. (*screams, jumps backward, overwhelmed with confusion,
and gasps for breath as she speaks*) Oh, gracious goodness, how
you frightened me ! I beg—your—pardon—sir—I—thought—I—
thought——

Judge. (*calmly*) That I was not around !

Dolly. (*humbly*) I hope—I have not offended you——

Judge. Oh, no, certainly not ! To whom were you talking ?
(*goes to table and faces audience*)

Dolly. (*scans room quickly, eyes rest a moment upon* JULIUS *at
C. D., who gesticulates wildly to her not to tell*) Excuse—me—
sir—(*curtsies*) but—I—*think* I must have been talking to you.
(JULIUS *listens attentively, as he hears* DOLLY'S *reply, rubs hands
and gesticulates his thanks*)

Judge. (*looks steadily a moment at* DOLLY, *who hangs her head
and plays confusedly with cloth—*JULIUS *moves slightly L., so that
the* JUDGE *cannot see him—watches him sharply and disappears L.,
as soon as he gives his orders*) That will do, now, (*pointing to* C. D.)
leave the room ! (DOLLY *curtsies, starts, then hesitates*)

Dolly. (*humbly*) I hope, sir—(JULIUS *peeps in*)

Judge. (*explosively*) Go ! (JULIUS *jumps back* L., *as though
struck—*DOLLY *starts, then quickly* exits C. D., *frightened—*
JUDGE *watches her exit, then slowly facing audience, drops his
head one moment in thought, then speaks in measured tones*) Servants are proverbial for their frankness when released from all re-
straint, and under such circumstances, one need never sigh, "Oh,
for the gift to see ourselves as others see us ! " I never knew until
a moment ago that I was devoid of stability of purpose, and was
(*imitates* DOLLY'S *tone of voice*) a cross, snappish, surly old *brute!*
Ah, well ! what is the use of——

Enter HANSELL, C. D., *ushered in by* JULIUS.

Julius. (*bowing*) Mr. Hansell, sah. (*bows and* exits C. D.)

Hansell. (*advancing*) I believe you *sent* for me, sir——

Judge. Yes, but it is unnecessary for you to remind me of my
harshness to you yesterday, by emphasizing my *sending* for you.

Hansell. (*bowing*) Pardon me then for doing so.

Judge. In fact, I am heartily sorry for the manner in which I ordered you out of my house, and the annoyance you were subjected to by your false arrest. I *sent* for you for the purpose of apologizing for my lack of courtesy, and to thank you for the nobility of character you displayed in saving my home from destruction.

Hansell. Apologies are useless and thanks unnecessary. My *duty* was plain.

Judge. And you performed it like a man. You proved yourself, though you be but a mechanic, one of nature's noblemen! There—(*extending hand*) is my hand; if I have not offended you *too* deeply, accept it as an evidence that your manliness extends *even* to the forgiveness of your most bitter enemy.

Hansell. (*grasping his hand*) I never refuse a hand offered in friendship or in penitence.

Judge. Thank you. Now, Hansell, I had a double object in wanting to see you. I intend immediately to rebuild my mill destroyed last night, and to you I offer its superintendency as a reward for your fidelity to my interests.

Hansell. (*surprised*) To *me*, sir?

Judge. Yes, that is what I said.

Hansell. Really, sir, I hardly know how to thank you.

Judge. (*drily*) Then don't attempt it.

Hansell. I meant it——

Judge. (*interrupting*) Never mind what you meant. That's all right; I understand. I suppose you will accept the trust?

Hansell. Yes, sir,—or, rather, conditionally.

Judge. Name your conditions.

Hansell. That you will allow me to re-engage the men formerly in your employ.

Judge. (*surprised*) What! the men who burned my mill?

Hansell. Yes, sir,——

Judge. The men who tried to fire my residence?

Hansell. The same,——

Judge. And would not have hesitated to take my life had it been exposed to their fury!

Hansell. The truth of that I cannot vouch for; but remember, sir, in your *future* dealings with those men, the desperate straits to which they were driven, and *your own* participation in their crime of last night.

Judge. (*surprised*) I do not understand you. Do you charge me with being an accessory to their crime of arson?

Hansell. I do; for by your repeated refusals to grant their entreaties for work, unless they renounced their birthright by signing slavish articles of agreement, you *drove* them to starvation and frenzy, closed their eyes to all sense of honor, excited the demon of revenge within their breasts and furnished the venomous oil of malice that lighted the torch of destruction.

Judge. You are putting the case pretty strongly, Hansell.

Hansell. But not stronger than the facts warrant.

Judge. (*sternly*) I do not wish to be insulted in my own house.

Hansell. (*quickly*) I do not wish to insult you, but I *do* desire that you may see yourself as others see you.

Judge. (*irritated*) Thank you. I well know how I appear to others. (*aside*) Dolly informed me. (*aloud*) Is there no other condition upon which you will accept the position offered you?

Hansell. Absolutely none. My lot is cast with my fellow workmen's, and if you cannot extend your kindness to them, you debar *me* from accepting it.

Judge. Are you in earnest?

Hansell. I am, sir. My word of honor is at stake.

Judge. For the sake of a foolish sentiment of honor, will you allow a lucrative position to slip through your grasp?

Hansell. (*looks at him a moment*) I would permit a *kingdom* to slip through it, rather than prove a *traitor* to my fellow workmen, and *false* to my sworn obligations.

Judge. (*musing*) You are a strange being!

Hansell. Perhaps I am, but it is better to be warm-hearted, forgiving and *true* to your fellow-men, than to be the monarch of the universe and devoid of principle.

Judge. If I thought there were others in your order who hold to *your* lofty ideas of *true* manhood, I might be tempted to accept your conditions.

Hansell. (*quickly*) There *are* others—hundreds of them—truer, better and nobler men than I, who see the folly of their hasty action in striking, and only await your pleasure to acknowledge their error and make you what amends they can. Oh, sir, if you would add brilliancy to the glorious sunlight of this morning and fill the air with gladness and song, accept *my* condition.

Judge. If I consent to the re-engagement of my former men, it must be at your expense.

Hansell. (*quickly*) In what way?

Judge. By the loss of the position I offered you a moment ago.

Hansell. I will cheerfully submit to that, knowing the joy my sacrifice will bring to many an aching heart.

Judge. There *need be* no sacrifice. Your willingness dispenses with the necessity of it. I agree to *your* terms, and thank you, too, for teaching me that there is something else in life worth living for than self.

Hansell. (*eagerly*) Then you promise to take back all the men formerly in your employ?

Judge. I do, without exception, and you can now go and inform them of the fact.

Hansell. (*grasping his hand*) Thank you, sir. Were you *my own father* I could not feel *prouder* of you than I do at this moment. Now I can go forth and *prove* to my companions that my action last night was for their best interest—*traitor* though they thought me then. (*speaks rapidly*) I cannot express my gratitude to you, sir, nor that of the men whose homes will be the brighter for the assurance of future aid from you. May Heaven's blessing rest upon you—will be the prayers offered by many a mother this day——

Judge. There, there, that will do! Now go.

Hansell. (*going*) I will, but let me hope that Labor and Capital, once more united, may never again become estranged, and that the pleasure you have this day conferred upon *others*, may reverberate through *your* heart and crown with a halo of happiness the remainder of your life.   Exit C. D.

Judge. (*facing audience, musingly*) There is not another man living who could have caused me to make such a dunce of myself. In fact, I was a *fool* for allowing him to cajole me into making that rash promise. I will call him back, for I *cannot* keep it. I have sworn to break the stubborn will of those men, and I'll do it! (*starts quickly for* C. D. *talking, stops when near it, faces audience and stands* C.) I will show that impudent minx of a Dolly, and the world besides, that I have a will of my own, and when I say I'll *do* a thing, I *will* do it.

Enter LAURA C. D., *joyously, as the* JUDGE *utters* "I will do it—" *stands* R. *of* JUDGE.

Laura. Of *course* you will do it!

Judge. (*abruptly*) Will do what?

Laura. (*confused*) Why—ah! (*quickly*) What you said you would.

Judge. And pray what was that?

Laura. Really, sir—I can't—recall it just now, but I'm sure (*archly*) *you* remember it.

Judge. (*admiringly*) You do, eh? You are a sly puss! Did you mean what I said about my men?

Laura. (*quickly*) Yes, sir; that was it!

Judge. So I *will* do what I said, that is, perhaps I will. My dear, (*leads her back of table*) I wish to ask your advice about a little matter.

Laura. (*affecting surprise*) *My* advice, sir?

Judge. Yes, dear, *your* advice. Suppose, now, you had a number of men working for you, and they asked you to pay them more for their work than you could afford to, what would you do?

Laura. I would tell them that it was impossible.

Judge. Just so. Now, suppose they were to strike, that is, leave your employ in a body, what would you do then?

Laura. I would call them together in a body, present *figures* to prove I could not grant their request, reason with them about the injustice of their action, and *ask them to return to work.*

Judge. You would, eh?

Laura. Certainly. That would be the only manly course to pursue.

Judge. Ah! yes, perhaps it would, but *business* men don't usually look at it in that light.

Laura. I am aware that *some* (*significantly*) do not, more's the pity.

Judge. (*wincing*) There is no need of your becoming *personal;* we were only *supposing* a case, you know.

Laura. Oh, excuse me. Now I understand. (*smiles aside*)

Judge. Yes, that's all right. Now, we'll take it for granted that you become incensed at the action of your men and close up your place of business. Your men in turn become angry with you and out of a feeling of revenge, set fire to your place of business and burn it down. What would you do then?

Laura. (*with animation, speaks rapidly*) Just let me tell you what *I* would do. If my men had asked me to let them resume work at their old wages and *I refused*, and they *then* set fire to my property, I should feel that I was a party to their crime, do you see?

Judge. Yes, yes——

Laura. Feeling that way, I should immediately rebuild my works, employ all my old hands and thus atone for my sin by forgiving them their's——

Judge. (*eagerly*) Would you really do that?

Laura. I would, sir; most assuredly.

Judge. But think of the expense you would be put to.

Laura. One should never take into account *dollars* and *cents* when he seeks forgiveness for wrong doing.

Judge. (*enthusiastically*) Laura, you are a trump! Excuse me, I do not mean that—I mean you speak my sentiments exactly.

Laura. (*eagerly*) Then you will rebuild your mill?

Judge. Yes——

Laura. And employ *all* your former hands?

Judge. (*becoming animated*) Yes, every one of them. Hansell I shall make——

Laura. What?

Judge. Superintendent of my mill——

Laura. (*clapping her hands*) Oh, you dear, good love of a man, I feel like kissing you!

Judge. (*gallantly*) Do it, my dear, I have not the least objection.

Laura. I believe I will (*starts for the* JUDGE, *is about to throw her arms around him when* enter HANS *quickly,* C. D.)

Hans. Meester——(*sees* LAURA *and the* JUDGE, *raises both hands*) Dunder und blitzen ! (*rushes out* C. D.—LAURA *and* JUDGE *separate*)

Judge. (*irritated*) Confound that stupid Dutchman !

Laura. (*suppressing a laugh*) Excuse me, sir, I will see what he wanted. (*goes rapidly to* C. D.)

Judge. (*coaxingly*) Stop a moment, dear. Come back, I wish to speak to you about that matter we were discussing yesterday morning.

Laura. (*smiling*) Some other time. You really *must* excuse me now. Exit, C. D.

Judge. (*pacing stage*) Hang that blockhead ! What business had *he* to enter unannounced ? What business has *any* servant, in fact ? They are a nuisance, an abomination, a set of tattlers who feed upon gossip and their employer's pocketbook. The whole kit of them are a diabolical set of sharks.

Enter JULIUS, C. D.

Julius. (*bowing*) 'Scuse me, sah, but yo' didn't want fur to see Mr. Thomas dis mornin', did yo' ?

Judge. (*savagely*) No, I don't, nor anybody else. Get out of my sight !

Julius. I jest knowed it !

Judge. (*halting*) You knew what ?

Julius. Dat yo' didn't want fur to see him !

Judge. How did you know it ?

Julius. 'Kase yo' tole me.

Judge. When ?

Julius. Why, only a minnit ago.

Judge. (*starting for him angrily*) I'll——

Julius. (*starting to run off*) No, yo' won't——

Judge. (*halting*) Where is Thomas ?

Julius. (*near door*) In de entry, jist outside de do' dar. (*pointing out,* C. D.)

Judge. (*angrily*) Well ! What are you standing there for ? Why don't you show him in ?

Julius. 'Kase yo' told me not to.

Judge. I told you nothing of the kind.

Julius. Yo' did, sah, sartin'.

Judge. What do you *mean* by *contradicting* me ?

Julius. I'se like to know wot yo' mean yo'se'f ? When I axes yo' if yo' wanted fur to see Mr. Thomas yo' said—" *No !* "

Judge. (*angrily, walking to table*) I'll show you what I meant in two seconds, you impudent rascal, if you don't show him in here immediately !

Julius. (*going to* C. D.) Why can't yo' say wot yo' *mean* i:
fust place, an' *stick* to it? A fellah nebber knows how to took
(*to* THOMAS) Come in, sah. (**enter** THOMAS, C. D.) Mr. Thor
sah.   **Exit** C. D., *but reappears and peeps in throughout scen*

Thomas. (*bowing*) Good morning, sir.

Judge. (L. *of table, curtly*) We'll dispense with all formali
sir. Proceed to state your business. What brought you here

Thomas. The desire to make an explanation——

Judge. In regard to what?

Thomas. My conduct of yesterday.

Judge. Entirely unnecessary. You deliberately assaulte
guest of mine in this room, outraged my hospitality, and subje
me to the mortification of prosecuting an innocent man. He.
forth, we are strangers.

Thomas. But, Judge, if I prove the assault was made in
interest——

Judge. (*incredulous*) In *my* interest!

Thomas. In behalf of the sanctity of your fireside——

Judge. In what way?

Thomas. To protect your home and honor against the mach
tions of an unprincipled man.

Judge. (*sarcastically*) Your action would be most remarkab

Thomas. Well, sir, such are the facts of the case, and I l
to your good judgment the decision as to whether I have pr
myself your friend or your foe.

Judge. The *facts* of the case, as related by you, contain noth.
Explain yourself.

Thomas. You know a mechanic by the name of Hansell, I
lieve?

Judge. I do.

Thomas. That is, you *think* you do. Have you ever tested his
principles?

Judge. I have, and found them to be of the *very* best quality.

Thomas. Do you know anything of his antecedents?

Judge. Absolutely nothing.

Thomas. I thought not. Did you ever watch him closely,
secretly?

Judge. No.

Thomas. Have you never noticed a certain uneasiness about
him at times, as though something were troubling him?

Judge. Now you recall it, I believe I have.

Thomas. Did you ever perceive him start and glance hastily
around, as though expecting some unseen foe to attack him?

Judge. I have, frequently.

Thomas. And wondered, no doubt, what caused it?

Judge. That's true.

Thomas. Yet you never attempted, by questioning him, to learn the cause, did you?

Judge. Yes, on one or two occasions, while he was working in the mill.

Thomas. With what result?

Judge. With the result of overwhelming him with confusion.

Thomas. As I thought. That man has a guilty conscience. I dare not *speak* of his heinous crime, yet conscience ever reproaches him with his sin, and denies him peace of mind.

Judge. (*surprised*) Why, what do you mean?

Thomas. Judge, you believe that man to be honorable?

Judge. I do.

Thomas. Incapable of deceit?

Judge. More so than most men.

Thomas. Possessed of the most sterling principles of virtue, honor and forbearance?

Judge. A man among a thousand!

Thomas. A man devoid of hatred and malice?

Judge. Perfectly so.

Thomas. One who loves his fellow creatures?

Judge. With as pure a love as that of angels.

Thomas. Who would not be guilty of shedding human blood?

Judge. No, sir—*never!*

Thomas. And yet, by the pale moon's dim light, I have seen him clasp a pure innocent girl by the throat and throttle her till life was extinct!

Judge. (*horrified*) What!

Thomas. 'Tis true. As he flung her lifeless form among the breakers on the beach, and stood there with his face wreathed in a smile of diabolical hatred, he looked like a fiend incarnate. Do you remember the case of Lillian Duer?

Judge. The girl who was murdered at Swansville, some three years ago?

Thomas. The same.

Judge. I do.

Thomas. She was his victim!

Judge. That cannot be.

Thomas. Was not the man who was arrested for the crime, named Hansell?

Judge. I believe so.

Thomas. And *your* Hansell entered your employ—when?

Judge. A little over two years ago.

Thomas. Just so. He was driven from his former home by the indignation of his neighbors, about that time, and settled here.

Judge. Can it be possible? He was tried for the crime, was he not?

Thomas. He was.

Judge. You saw him commit the deed?

Thomas. I did.

Judge. He was acquitted?

Thomas. Yes.

Judge. You were a witness against him?

Thomas. I was.

Judge. Then how was he freed?

Thomas. By the perjured evidence of his mother and sister, who swore he never left his home the night of the murder.

Judge. Was there no other evidence than yours offered against him?

Thomas. ·Yes. Footprints leading to and from the body were found to correspond exactly to the shoes worn by Hansell.

Judge. Then there was no doubt of Hansell's guilt, provided his mother and sister swore falsely?

Thomas. None whatever. So general was the belief in his guilt, that had he remained in town another week he would have been lynched.

Judge. And this is the man I thought so noble and true!

Thomas. Now, Judge, imagine my feelings when I met that man—a murderer—yesterday in this room, seemingly enjoying the freedom of your house.

Judge. I cannot!

Thomas. I felt assured you were not aware of his true character, else you would discourage the intimacy existing between him and your ward.

Judge. (*astounded*) What's that? *He intimate* with Laura?

Thomas. That's what I said.

Judge. Why, man, they don't know each other.

Thomas. (*significantly*) Don't they? You must be blind!¦

Judge. Blind to what?

Thomas. The affection existing between them. Why, it is known all over town.

Judge. I do not believe it.

Thomas. Perhaps not. Yet it was to save you the disgrace of that knowledge, that I quarreled with Hansell yesterday.

Judge. (*excited*) Laura does *not* love Hansell!

Thomas. I tell you she does.

Judge. It's false! I guess I know *whom* she loves.

Thomas. Perhaps you think so.

Judge. I tell you *I do* know! Don't you contradict me again, sir.

Thomas. Certainly not, yet I can't help feeling sorry for you. .

Judge. Sorry for *me!*

Thomas. Yes, sir.

Judge. Why?

Thomas. Because of the deception being practiced upon you.

Judge. By whom?

Thomas. Hansell and Miss Laura.

Judge. (*irritated*) I tell you, you are mistaken. Don't you suppose I know? (*with importance*) Laura loves *me*, sir!

Thomas. (*astonished*) You, sir?

Judge. Yes, *me*. Is there anything astonishing in that?

Thomas. No, nothing particularly. (*aside*) I understand now. (*aloud*) Did she ever say so?

Judge. Not in so many words, but her actions plainly showed it.

Thomas. (*significantly*) I suppose *Hansell* thinks the same.

Judge. (*angrily*) Hansell be d——. (*quickly*) What do I care what *he* thinks?

Thomas. Perhaps you *would* care, if you were to see him and your ward together.

Judge. (*startled*) He and Laura together! When? Where?

Thomas. At his home. I saw them there only last night.

Judge. At what time?

Thomas. Just after Hansell's release.

Judge. Ah! I see. *Now* I know why she hurried away from the magistrate's and left *me*. So she meets that reprobate secretly, does she?

Thomas. Yes, but it is *his* fault.

Judge. (*furiously*) I know it is, the contemptible scoundrel, the low-bred——(*abruptly*) Are you *sure* it is *Laura* who meets him?

Thomas. I *am* sure of it. If you doubt my word you can see for yourself, for I'll——

Judge. (*excitedly, pacing stage*) No, you won't. I don't want to *see*. What in the dickens do *I* want to *see* another man caressing the woman I love for? Are you a fool? Do you think me one? Are your senses gone? To think that Laura, whom I thought pure and innocent, guilty of such deception! It is too much—too much!

Thomas. (*trying to pacify him*) There, there, Judge, be calm. *She* is not at fault. *Hansell* is the one to blame. ·

Judge. That's true, *he's* the one, the mean, sneaking, low-principled assassin! Why in thunder didn't you kill him yesterday?

Thomas. I dared not. Now that you know his baseness, I trust you will no longer condemn me for assaulting him.

Judge. Condemn you! I never did. I always knew *you* were a gentleman. You did right—(*shakes* THOMAS' *hand*) and I honor you for it. As for that Hansell, I'll send him a note and have a settlement in full with him this very day. (enter NEB, C. D., *dressed dudishly, followed by* MESSRS. THOMPKINS *and* SQUASH) Visitors, confound them! (THOMAS *goes up* L., *as* NEB *speaks*)

Neb. (*bowing*) Massa Thompkins and Massa Squash, sah. (JUDGE *salutes guests pleasantly*)

Thomas. (*going*) I will see you again this afternoon. Good-morning, sir.

Judge. Be sure and do so; but, wait, I will accompany you to the door. (*to guests*) Excuse me for a moment. Neb, tell Julius to bring in some wine, and see that the gentlemen are made comfortable.   Exit *with* THOMAS, C. D.

Neb. Yes, sah. (*places chairs* R. *and* L. *of table*) Be seated gem'-men, an' make yourselves free an' easy. (*going*) I will order *our sarvent*, (*makes a wry face;* JULIUS *peeps in* C. D., *looks savagely, and shakes fist at* NEB, *but disappears* L. *before* NEB *turns*) to bring yo' in some wine. (*bows and* exits C. D.)

Thompkins. (*seated* L. *of table*) As I was saying when I entered, the Judge was much more passionate in his younger days than he is now.

Squash. (R.) Ah, indeed!

Thompkins. Yes, his wife ran away from him—or rather his brutality *drove* her away.

Squash. (*astonished*) His wife?

Thompkins. Didn't you know he had been married?

Squash. No.

Thompkins. What?

Squash. It's a fact.

Thompkins. She left him one night over twenty years ago.

Squash. You don't say so!

Thompkins. And took her two children, a boy and girl, with her.

Squash. Do tell!

Thompkins. The affair created quite a stir at the time.

Squash. No doubt of it.

Thompkins. A regular *breeze*, in fact, for it blew the Judge out of Roxford and landed him here.

Squash. You don't say so! But what became of his wife?

Thompkins. She died some ten years ago.

Squash. And the children?

Thompkins. The Lord only knows. No one, not even the Judge, could ever find out. But, hush! here comes the Judge.

Re-enter JUDGE C. D., *takes seat behind table*—JULIUS *follows him, bearing tray, with two bottles of wine and three wine glasses; appears indignant*—NEB *follows him to* C. D., *elated*—JULIUS *places bottles and glasses upon table, goes up* C., *tosses tray on sofa, and stands directly back of* JUDGE—*when he and his guests begin to drink,* JULIUS *takes bottle from breast pocket and does likewise, never removing his gaze from the* JUDGE.

Judge. Ah, gentlemen, judging from the animated tone of your conversation, I should say *my* presence was not missed. (*sits*)

Squash. (*with emphasis*) Not at all, not at *all,* sir !

Judge. (*looks hard at* SQUASH *a moment ; drily*) Thank you. (*half rises*) Perhaps it would have been more agreeable to you if I had remained out altogether.

Squash. (*confused*) Excuse—me—Judge, do not leave—sit still —I meant—I meant—to——

Thompkins. (*quickly*) He meant to convey the impression that *considering* your absence we got along remarkably well.

Squash. (*quickly*) Yes, that's it. (*to* THOMPKINS) Thank you. (*to* JUDGE) You really must excuse me, Judge.

Judge. (*interrupting, smiles*) Certainly, sir. Your embarrassment proves that you meant no offence. Here, gentlemen, (*hands each a bottle*) is some grape wine over six years old, that I would like you to try. Help yourselves. We'll dispense with ceremony. (*fills glasses*)

Julius. (*holding up bottle, aside*) An' here's de remnant ob de champagne. We'll 'spense wid ceremony, too. Here's lookin' at yo'. (*is about to place bottle to mouth, when* NEB *sneaks up behind him and snatches bottle out of his hand, guying* JULIUS, *who shows fight—*NEB *makes feint to strike him with bottle—*JULIUS *retreats, stands a moment pouting, then brightens up with an idea and runs out rapidly* C. D.—NEB *appears joyous,—drinks*)

Thompkins. (*drinking*) That's splendid !

Squash. (*draining glass*) I never tasted better. (*re-fills glass, smiling*) Excuse me.

Judge. That's right. Help yourself.

Squash. (*fervently*) Thank you, thank you. I am doing so, as you see. There's nothing *like* making yourself *at home,* and being free and easy under all circumstances.

Judge. That's true. It adds to our pleasure and dispenses with the necessity of formality. We are old friends who know one another well, and never meet but to enjoy ourselves. Eh, Thompkins ?

Re-enter JULIUS C. D. ; *has bottles sticking out* R. *and* L. *pockets, demijohn in hand—takes former position—makes a face at* NEB *and drinks from demijohn, evincing pleasure—watches* JUDGE *closely.*

Thompkins. Yes, sir, you hit the nail square on the head that time. Our motto is when together, " Drink and be merry."

Squash. (*helping himself*) Thanks, I have no objection whatever. (THOMPKINS *and* JUDGE *laugh*)

Judge. (*pointing to* SQUASH) An offspring of a *crawler,* becoming merry at the expense of a *climber!* (*laughs*)

Thompkins. (*appears not to comprehend at first*) Ah, yes ! (*suddenly*) By jove, not so bad, Judge. I didn't see the point at first. (*laughs*) A *Squash* feeding on *grapes.*

Neb *quietly placing bottle on sofa, steals bottles from* Julius' *pockets—placing them beside others, he returns and snatches demijohn from* Julius—*commences to drink from it, guarding sofa*—Julius *appears crestfallen, then grins and searches pockets; finding bottles gone, he approaches* Neb *and engages him in an animated dumb conversation, features and form depicting anger, gesticulating with rapidity.*

Squash. All right, gentlemen. Enjoy yourselves at my expense as much as you can. (*refills glasses*) I'm perfectly happy. (*if talent will permit, holds glass aloft and commences singing the chorus of the Drinking Song from " Giroflé Girofla"*—Judge *and* Thompkins *joining, with glasses raised*—Neb *and* Julius *seize each other and commence tussling*)

Thompkins. (*at conclusion of song*) That burst of melody from our friend reminds me, Judge, that the last time we were here, you promised to make Neb sing for us. I believe that was the agreement, wasn't it, Squash?

Squash. Certainly, and we expect the Judge to redeem his promise.

Judge. All right, gentlemen, I will do so. (*turning, calls*) Julius! (*sees him and* Neb *butting each other*) What in thunder are you boys doing? (Thompkins *nudges* Squash; *both look at boys and laugh; boys separate*)

Julius. He was 'posing on me again. I'll bust his old cocoanut for him yet, see if I don't.

Neb. (*angrily*) Yo' can't do it, yo' black Guinea nigger!

Judge. There, there, boys, that will do. Come here, Neb. I wish you to sing for these gentlemen. Will you do it?

Thompkins. (*handing him money*) There's a half dollar for you to buy your girl some taffy with, if you sing.

Neb. (*bows, takes coin, laughs*) T'ank you, sah, but my gal dun need for me to *buy* her taffy. She jest t'inks I'se a barrel of m'lasses myself. (*to* Judge, *with alacrity*) Sartinly I'll sing, but wot am it to be, Massa?

Judge. Oh, that new piece you were singing the other night.

Neb. Oh, yes, I know. All right, sah. Yo' just tune up de music, while I gits my hat and cane. (*runs out* C. D.—Judge *goes to organ and plays a prelude*—Julius *goes down and stands* L. I *wing*—Squash *turns chair and faces audience, holding glass in* L. *hand, leaning back in chair*—Thompkins *seizes bottle and keeps* Squash's *glass full during song*)

Julius. (*speaks through music, contemptuously*) Dat niggah am de conceitedest feller dat ebber lived. He can't sing. I can knock de stuffin' out ob him in dat line any day. (re-enter Neb C. D.; *has silk hat on and cane tucked under arm; assumes a dudish air*) Look at him! He's degustin'!

NEB. (*coming* C.) I'se ready. (*to audience*) Dis am my new suit.

Song and chorus introduced—walks up and down front ; every time he approaches JULIUS *he assumes a tantilizing air—*JULIUS *is first irritated, then mad, and finally gets into a passion—makes feint to strike* NEB, *who threatens him with cane—at conclusion of first verse and chorus* JULIUS *exclaims*

Julius. (*aside*) Dem am de clothes he got wid de money he stole from me. I don't care if I nebber speak to him again.

NEB *sings second verse and chorus—at conclusion* THOMPKINS *and* SQUASH *applaud vigorously—*JUDGE *continues to play a few bars —if there is no encore* NEB *approaches* JULIUS *who has been intently gazing at hat worn by* NEB, *who makes a face at him—* JULIUS *snatches hat off* NEB *as he comes near him.*

Neb. (*in undertone, threateningly*) Mind what yo' am about, niggah !
Julius. (*in undertone, angrily*) What yo' mean by wearin' *my* hat fur?
Neb. (*increasing tone*) Kase I wanted to.
Julius. (*raising voice*) Yo' had better not do it ag'in. (*in this scene* NEB *and* JULIUS *increase the tone of voice in each passage until both become thoroughly angry*)
Neb. I will if I want to.
Julius. No, yo' won't.
Neb. Yo' can't hinder me.
Julius. Yo' see wedder I kin or no.
Neb. We *will* see. Gib me dat hat ag'in.
Julius. I won't.
Neb. Gib it to me, I say.
Julius. I sha'n't.
Neb. Gib it to me, 'fore I kick de crown off it.
Julius. If yo' kick dis hat yo' have got me fur to lick.
Neb. I'll do it, suah, if yo' don't fork it over.
Julius. Keep away from me, niggah.
Neb. Don't yo' be callin' me names, or I'll lam yo' right here 'fore dese gem'men.
Julius. Yo' can't do it.
Judge. (*rises from instrument, sees* JULIUS *and* NEB *quarreling —*THOMPKINS *and* SQUASH *have been silently enjoying the scene*) What in the deuce is the matter with you boys, *now ?* (JULIUS *and* NEB *go* C., *back of table quickly ; both talk rapidly to* JUDGE)
Julius. He wus tryin' to make me gib him my hat.
Neb. He snatched it right of'en my head widout axin' fur it.
Julius. He's no business wearin' ob it.

Neb. I 'tend to wear it wheneber I feels 'clined to, Mr. Niggah.

Julius. Dem clothes he bought wid the money he *stole* frum me.

Neb. Dat's a lie.

Julius. It am de gospel truth, Massa.

Neb. Even if I did, it am not half as bad as pickin' Massa's pockets.

Julius. *Who* picked Massa's pockets?

Neb. Yo' did!

Julius. (*shaking fist under* NEB's *nose*) I'll make yo' prove dat 'fore a 'Squire.

Neb. Yo' hab me 'rested if yo' dare.

Julius. Den yo'll have to take dat 'sinuation back.

Neb. I'll not do it, an' de likes ob yo' can't make me, either.

Julius. But yo'll *hab* to do it.

Neb. (*close to him*) Who'll make me?

Julius. I will.

Neb. Do it *now!* Yo's 'fraid, yo' am a coward.

Squash. Go for him, Julius. Don't take that.

Julius. I don't 'tend to. (*strikes* NEB, *clinch and tussle*—THOMPKINS *rises, all laugh*—SQUASH *attempts to rise, upsets chair and falls over*—JUDGE *and* THOMPKINS *clap hands*—SQUASH *rises, seems a little unsteady*)

Judge. There, boys, that will do.

T. *and* **S.** (*in unison*) No, no, let them go.

Judge. All right then, fight it out.

Thompkins. I'll bet on Neb.   .

Squash. Julius is my boy. Go for him, Julius. If you lick him, I'll give you a dollar. (JUDGE, THOMPKINS *and* SQUASH *evince much pleasure*)

Thompkins. (*going behind* NEB) Squash, second *your* man. (SQUASH *goes behind* JULIUS) Judge, you act as referee and time-keeper. (*the boys separate*, NEB L., JULIUS R.; *stand panting and glaring at each other*—THOMPKINS *and* SQUASH *urge them on—they approach and strike without effect*—NEB *rushes at* JULIUS *who steps aside*—NEB *plants both fists in* SQUASH's *stomach, which floors him*—JULIUS *rushes at* NEB, *who stops him*—NEB *throws right arm back and knocks over* THOMPKINS, *who falls across doorway* C.)

Enter HANS, *hurriedly*, C. D.

Hans. Meester——(*trips over* THOMPKINS *and falls forward—springing quickly to feet, he darts a hurried glance around room—sees* NEB *and* JULIUS *tussling up* C., *goes for them, snatches them apart and hits them on side of head; is raving mad*) You dinks you be schmart: putty soon you dink——

Julius. (*rushing at* Hans) Come on, Neb, (*both attack* Hans *and drive him up* c.—Julius *strikes* Hans *on stomach and bursts a bladder concealed under his clothing*—Hans *falls on stomach*)

Neb. (*at* Hans' *feet*) Sour krout has taken a tumble !

Julius. (*mounting* Hans' *shoulders*) De war am ended. Germany has fallen. De *world* am our *own !* (Judge R. 1 E.; Squash R. 2 E.; Thompkins L. 1 E.; Neb L. 2 E.; Julius *standing on* Hans' *shoulders*)

QUICK DROP.

———

ACT IV.

Scene.—*Same as Act III. Front part of organ is moved slightly away from wing, displaying* Neb *secreted behind it—top of* Julius' *head is seen projecting above sofa,* L.—*as curtain rises* Laura *steps in from* c. d., *looks around room, and advances a few steps down* c., *talking to herself, holding in* R. *hand a letter sealed and stamped—lively music.*

Laura. I wonder where those boys are ! (Neb *and* Julius *peep at her from hiding places*) I have searched this house over and can't find them anywhere. It is too bad. I want this letter mailed, (*holding up letter*) and there is no one to take it to the office. I do wish there was some system used in running this house, then perhaps there would be more regularity in the attendance of our servants.

Enter DOLLY, C. D.

Dolly, have you seen Neb or Julius lately ?

Dolly. No, ma'am, not since dinner.

Laura. Have you any idea where I would be likely to find one of them?

Dolly. No, indeed. Meal hour is the only time one can feel *certain* as to *their* whereabouts.

Laura. If you come across either one of them, send him to my room. I have an errand I wish performed.   Exit C. D.

Dolly. Yes, ma'am, I will. It's a shame the way the Judge allows those boys to neglect their work. He has lost all control over them, and yet, they are not such bad boys after all—full of mischief, and——

Julius. (*behind sofa*) Hoop !

DOLLY, *startled, looks toward sofa*—NEB *peeps over organ at her, raises putty blower to mouth, and shoots* DOLLY *on side of head— she starts and brushes object away.*

Dolly. What was that? (*looks* R.; JULIUS *shoots her; she turns* L.; NEB *blows again; turns* R., *then* JULIUS *shoots; turns* L., *then quickly* R., *sees* NEB'S *head, walks to instrument*) Oh, ho; so it was you !

Neb. (*coming from hiding place*) Whar's Hans?

Julius. (L.) Yes, whar is he?

Dolly. Why, how do I know?

Neb. We thought he wuz comin' in here.

Dolly. So you were hiding, to surprise him?

Julius. Yes, we 'tended to gib him 'ticular fits.

Dolly. Didn't you hear Miss Laura asking for you two?

Neb. No, we closed our ears.

Julius. Say, you ought to hab seen me an' Neb do up Hans dis mornin' !

Neb. Jule busted his wind fur him.

Dolly. "Busted his wind"? Why, what do you mean?

Neb. Why, he knocked him out ob time. Say, I'll show yo'. (*catches hold of* JULIUS, *pulls him* C. *and gets in front of him*) Yo', see dar (*pointing to* JULIUS) stood Hans. Now, I'se Jule. He doubled up his fists dis way, (*suit action*) an' rushed at Hans, an' hit him square in his stump-jack dis way. (*rushes at* JULIUS *who steps quickly aside;* NEB *falls flat on stomach*)

Julius. (*quickly, pointing at* NEB) And *down* he went jist like dat. (JULIUS *and* DOLLY *laugh*)

Neb. (*rises, crestfallen*) Yo' am a mean niggah to sarve me like dat !

Julius. Yo' don't suppose *I* wanted to be winded, did yo'?

Neb. (*rubbing himself*) Yo' might hab let me, it wouldn't hab hurted yo' much, anyhow.

Julius. No, sir, I'm not takin' nuffin like dat jist now. Say, (*eagerly to* DOLLY) does yo' want to see sum fun?

Dolly. Why?

Julius. If yo' does, jist go an' send Hans in dis room fur sumfin', an' den yo' come back an' peep in de do' dar. (*pointing* C. D.)

Dolly. Why, what are you going to do?

Julius. Nebber yo' mind. Yo'll see. We's 'pared to 'ceive him, ain't we, Neb?

Neb. Yes, siree, we'll warm his jacket fur him.

Dolly. (*going*) Promise you'll not hurt him if I send him in.

Neb. Oh, no, we'll not hurt him !

Julius. Ob course we won't !

Dolly. Very well, then, I'll do it.

Neb. Say, will yo' please do us anoder favor?

Dolly. What is it ?

Neb. Close de shutters ob dis room, so it am dark.   De light hurts my eyes.

Julius. By golly, but dat am an idea.   (*to* DOLLY)   Yo'll do it, won't yo' ?

Dolly. (*laughing*) Yes, I'll do that, too ; but, remember boys, Miss Laura wants one of you to do an errand for her.

Julius. All right.   *I'll* do it.   It won't take me two minnits to go to de office fur her.

Dolly. (*at* C. *door*) What office ?

Julius. De pos'-office.

Dolly. How do you know she wants you to go there ?

Julius. Hasn't she got a letter fur to mail ?

Dolly. Has she ?

Julius. Ob course she hab.

Dolly. How do you know ?

Julius. Didn't I heerd her say so ?

Dolly. When ?

Julius. Only a minnit ago, when she was in here.

Dolly. Then your ears were *not* closed, after all ?

Julius. (*making a face*) Yo' cotched me dat time, but I'll take dat letter all de same.

Dolly. Very well, see that you don't forget it.   Exit C. D.

Julius. Neb, dat wus a bully idea ob yo's, ter hab de shetters closed.   Whar did yo' git it ?

Neb. Out ob my head.

Julius. Go way from me.   Yo' did nuffin' ob de kind.

Neb. Ob course I did.

Julius. Yo' can't make me believe dat.

Neb. Why ?

Julius. 'Kase yo' am not got larnin' 'nough !

Neb. It does not 'quire larnin' to discog'tate a t'ing like dat.

Julius. No—o——

Neb. It am de 'sult ob de nat'ral 'specity ob de equi—liver—dum.

Julius. Oh, yes, now I un'stand.   But, say, Neb, hadn't we better be a sneakin' ? (*lights are gradually lowered*) See, Dolly am a closin' de shetters.

Neb. 'Spects we had. (*both return to hiding places, lights very low*)

Julius. Neb !

Neb. What ?

Julius. Am it dark ober dar ?

Neb. I should say so !

Julius. Is yo' 'fraid ?

Neb. No, ob course, I isn't.   Am yo' ?

Julius. No—but I feel sort of lonesome.   Say, Neb !

Neb. What am it?

Julius. Yo' won't run away, will yo'?

Neb. Ob course not.

Julius. Yo' will stick to me?

Neb. No matter wot turns up. But say, Jule!

Julius. Hush! he am a comin'.

Neb. Yo' can 'pend on me.

Julius. Hush!

Enter JUDGE C. D., *quickly*—JULIUS *and* NEB *attack him simultaneously, beating him over head with bladders covered with muslin.*

Judge. (*screaming*) Murder! robbers!

Exit L. D.—*boys come* C., *startled.*

Julius. By golly, Neb, *now* we's done it!

Neb. We hab, fur suah!

Julius. Did yo' know it wus de Jedge 'fore he hollered?

Neb. No.

Julius. I thought *he* wus Hans.

Neb. So did I.

Julius. Wot'll we do?

Neb. I dunno!

Julius. We had better skip!

Neb. Dat's so. (*both start for* C. D.; *when near it they stop and listen*)

Julius. Hush! sum one's comin'!

Neb. It am Hans.

Julius. Dat am so. Yo' git on one side ob de door an' I'll git on de oder, (*rubbing hands*) an' we'll gib him thunder! (JULIUS L., NEB R.)

Enter HANS C. D.; *has flour concealed in palm of hands*—JULIUS *and* NEB *attack him vigorously, beat him over head, face and shoulders, drive him* C.—HANS *places hands over face and gets flour in mouth, nose and eyes—the boys start for* C. D., *throw bladder bags in front of them, jump on them; they explode*—HANS *jumps; the boys pick up bags and* exeunt *quickly* C. D.

Enter JUDGE L. D. *with pistol—sees* HANS.

Judge. Surrender, you villain! (*discharges pistol*—HANS *screams and jumps*) Surrender, you scoundrel! (*fires; lights are up quickly*—HANS C.; *drops to knees, working eyes to get out flour; nose, eyes and mouth appear full of it*—JUDGE *goes to* HANS, *catches him by collar, lifts him up and applies boot, talking*)

Judge. (*in a rage*) You incorrigible Dutchman! How dare you assault me in my own house? I'll teach you a lesson you will not soon forget. How does that feel? (*kicking* HANS) And that? and that?

Enter JULIUS, C. D. *with blunderbuss followed by* NEB *and* DOLLY—
NEB *has a cleaver in his hand.*

Julius. Where am de assassin? Show me dem! (*pointing gun
around room*)

Neb. Jist let *me* git at dem. I'll make mince meat ob de blood-
thirsty varmints in two seconds. (DOLLY *stands up* C., *silently
laughing*)

Judge. (*violently shaking* HANS) Will you ever attempt another
trick like that on me? (HANS *attempts to speak*) Don't you open
your lips, or I'll discharge you on the spot.

Enter LAURA C. D., *in a state of trepidation.*

Laura. In heaven's name, what is the meaning of this uproar?
I heard pistol shots and a scream, and I thought some one was
being murdered.

Judge. And so there *was*; that is, an *attempt* was made to *murder
me.* (*places pistol in hip pocket*)

Laura. To murder you?

Judge. Yes, I was knocked down and beaten shamefully.

Laura. Where?

Judge. In this room.

Laura. Then it was *your* cries I heard?

Judge. Yes, I narrowly escaped with my life. By a superhuman
effort I released myself from the grasp of my assailant, hurled him
to the floor, ran out, got my revolver and returned in time to prevent his escape. (*delivered rapidly, with action*—NEB, JULIUS *and*
DOLLY *glance at one another and smile*)

Laura. Who was your assailant?

Judge. (*sternly*) Why, Hans there! (*pointing*)

Laura. Hans? (*the boys appear tickled*)

Hans. Meester Schudge!

Judge. Not a word!

Hans. But *I vill* say sumdings. You shust mistaken be!

Judge. About what?

Hans. Dot I strikes you!

Judge. Didn't I see you do it?

Hans. Nein!

Judge. What?

Hans. Nein, it vas some oder fellow. I vas almost kilt to deff
mein self.

Judge. You were?

Hans. Yah, und mein head shust feel like it vos stuffed mit snitz
und vasser, und it—all—(*perplexed*)

Julius. Sort o' swelled like?

Hans. (*quickly*) Yah, dot's so.

Judge. (*advancing angrily toward him,* HANS *retreating*) You lying scoundrel, get out of this room. You can't blarney me. (HANS *hesitates and attempts to speak*) Not another word, *go!* (*points* C. D., HANS exits *quickly*) I'll attend to your case later. Now I wish to know who closed the window shutters and what for? (*consternation seizes* DOLLY, NEB *and* JULIUS)

Julius. I 'spects it wus de wind dat blowed dem shet.

Neb. So do I.

Judge. *Why* do you? (NEB *is embarrassed*)

Julius. 'Kase when I opened dose on dat side (R.) dey wus not fastened.

Neb. Neider wus dose on dis side. (L.)

Judge. (*sarcastically*) No doubt the shutters closed themselves. I shall investigate this matter thoroughly and fix the blame where it belongs.

Julius. Well, I didn't tech de blamed old shetters.

Judge. (*angrily*) What do you *mean* by using such language in my presence?

Julius. Well, yo' needn't 'spicion in'cent pussons den.

Neb. (*to* JUDGE) I'se gibs yo' a week's notice. I'm a gwine to leave yo'r sarvice.

Julius. An' I too. I'se tired ob habin' my 'racity 'peached on ebbery 'casion.

Judge. (*emphatically*) You can leave *now* for all I care. Clear out of here, both of you—(*to* DOLLY) and you, too; I wish to see Miss Bell alone. (exeunt NEB *and* JULIUS C. D., *grumbling to themselves,* DOLLY *following, half laughing—*LAURA *hands her letter and points to boys—*DOLLY *nods head*)

Laura. Don't you think, sir, you are a little too severe upon the boys?

Judge. (*surly*) No, they deserve all they get.

Laura. Suppose they should leave you?

Judge. (*interrupting*) There is no danger of that. I couldn't *drive* them away. They have too easy a time of it here, and the rascals well know it. Now, Laura, (*goes to table, sits* L., LAURA *following to back of it*) I wish to ask you a few questions.

Laura. And I shall be most happy to answer them.

Judge. Don't be too sure of that.

Laura. Why not?

Judge. Wait and see. I have heard reports of you that are far from flattering.

Laura. (*surprised*) Why, what do you mean?

Judge. I believe you know a young mechanic by the name of Hansell?

Laura. The one who was here this morning?

Judge. The same.

Laura. I do.

Judge. (*slightly sneering*) A most estimable young man?

Laura. He is generally so considered.

Judge. Of incorruptible principles?

Laura. I believe so.

Judge. Worthy the love of even a *noble*-born woman?

Laura. That's true.

Judge. Incapable of deceit?

Laura. That's his reputation.

Judge. A fit associate for the pure and innocent?

Laura. Certainly, sir.

Judge. Of *course*. I was foolish to ask that question.

Laura. Why, sir?

Judge. Because your *actions* plainly show you so consider him.

Laura. I do not understand you.

Judge. Laura, you have deceived and grieved me beyond measure.

Laura. In what way?

Judge. By your indiscretion.

Laura. Why, what have I done?

Judge. You have caused yourself to become the target for the gossips of our town.

Laura. Indeed, sir, there must be some mistake. I am innocent of any wrong-doing.

Judge. Your *innocence* robs the blow, so far as you are concerned, of half its sting.

Laura. Again I ask what have I done? *How* have I deceived you?

Judge. By leading me to believe that you loved me, when your affections were centred upon another.

Laura. I have *not* deceived you, for I *do* love you dearly.

Judge. Ah!

Laura. Yes; sir, that's true.

Judge. (*aside, smiling*) I knew she couldn't resist me. (*aloud, pleasantly*) Well, my dear, that alters the case. Then you really love me?

Laura. I do.

Judge. Certainly you do. I am glad to hear you say so. You will never have cause to be sorry for it, Laura.

Laura. Thank you, sir, you have always been kind to me.

Judge. (*tenderly*) And *always* will be, dear. When *we* are married——

Laura. (*surprised*) Married, sir?

Judge. (*taken aback*) Yes, that is what I said.

Laura. *We?* You and *I*?

Judge. Certainly. Didn't I speak plainly enough?

Laura. Yes, but it seems so strange.

Judge. What's strange?

Laura. That you, who are old enough to be my father, should think of marrying.

Judge. It may seem strange, but I intend doing it.

Laura. But surely, sir, you will seek some one near your own age?

Judge. (*playfully*) Not unless *you* refuse me.

Laura. *I?* What have *I* to do with the case?

Judge. Oh, you little innocent dear! "What have *I* to do with the case?" (*laughs*) As if you don't know!

Laura. Indeed, sir, I don't.

Judge. Didn't you say you loved me?

Laura. I did.

Judge. Didn't I ask you to marry me?

Laura. No, sir!

Judge. I did, and you accepted me, too.

Laura. (*startled*) Indeed, sir, I did not. I misunderstood you.

Judge. (*nettled*) What! then you don't love me after all?

Laura. (*quickly*) Not in the sense you mean, but as a father.

Judge. (*quickly*) I do not want your love as a father—but as a husband.

Laura. That cannot be!

Judge. Why?

Laura. Because—(*hesitates*)

Judge. You love Hansell?

Laura. I did not say so.

Judge. No, not in so many words, but you might as well. Now let me tell you that the sooner you forget that man, the better it will be for all concerned, for *marry* him you *shall not.* I have been disgraced by you enough already.

Laura. Disgraced by me? In what way?

Judge. (*abruptly*) What do you mean by meeting Hansell secretly.

Laura. Who says I do?

Judge. Everybody. Your disgraceful conduct has become town talk. Only last night you visited his house and were seen talking to him.

Laura. Who told you that?

Judge. Never mind. Do you deny it?

Laura. I do not.

Judge. (*excitedly*) Then it is true?

Laura. It is.

Judge. (*sneeringly*) Yet you wonder "how you have deceived and grieved me," when you, whom I have reared as my own child, so far forget maidenly modesty as to force yourself upon the notice of that *low-born* fellow, who——

Laura. (*interrupting—speaks with power*) Stop! you have gone too far. Henry Hansell may be a "*low-born*" man, but he has never by word, look or action, attempted to insult a defenceless woman.

Judge. (*angrily*) Oh, ho! so you defend him?

Laura. As I would defend *you* were one to unjustly assail you!

Judge. And at my expense, too!

Laura. You left me no alternative.

Judge. (*excitedly*) Mark me, Laura, your cavalier Hansell is not what he seems to be.

Laura. He's as true a knight as ever wielded lance in defence of his country's honor!

Judge. (*passionately*) No doubt *you* think so. And yet, you shall see his lance broken in twain, and his proud plumes trailing in the dust of his dishonor.

Laura. Never! if he be shown fair play!

Judge. That he shall have, but his disgrace is inevitable. Before this day is over, I promise you he shall stand revealed in his true character. (enter THOMAS, C. D.) But leave me now, I will call you when I am ready for you.

Exit LAURA, C. D.—*as she passes* THOMAS *he bows—she looks at him searchingly—as she reaches* C. D., *she is met by* HANSELL—*they engage in earnest conversation outside* C. D., THOMAS *goes down* C.

Thomas. (*eagerly*) Has she heard yet?

Judge. No, but she soon shall. (*examines watch*) It is time he was here.

Thomas. How do you propose arranging matters?

Judge. I hardly know. (LAURA *aud* HANSELL *retreat* L. ; JUDGE *goes* R. *of organ*) I wish you, however, to sit here, (*down back of organ*) so as to be hidden from the gaze of Hansell. (THOMAS *crosses* R. *and takes seat as* JUDGE *stops speaking*) Your appearance on the scene is optional with you, but no doubt the dialogue will enable you to make it opportune.

Thomas. You can depend upon me, sir, to see that it *is*. (JUDGE *crosses to* L. *of table and sits*)

Judge. I have instructed Julius to show Hansell in here as soon as he comes, and to remain in the room, in case he is required to corroborate your statements.

Thomas. That was a wise move.

Judge. Hush!

Enter JULIUS, C. D., *followed by* HANSELL, *who has a letter in his hand.*

Julius. (*bowing*) Mr. Hansell. (*goes down* R.—HANSELL *goes down* C., *near table*)

Judge. (*coldly*) You are punctual.

Hansell. I always try to meet my appointments promptly.

Judge. That's good.

Hansell. And to treat all men fairly and honorably.

Judge. Better still.

Hansell. But it seems *I* am not to receive the same recognition.

Judge. Indeed!

Hansell. No, sir. What is the reason?

Judge. Pray, how do I know?

Hansell. You know why it is denied me in this letter. (*holding it up*)

Judge. I do not.

Hansell. Did you not write it? (*handing it to* JUDGE)

Judge. (*examines it*) I did.

Hansell. And yet you do not know *why* I am treated in it so unjustly?

Judge. That's true.

Hansell. In that letter you hint of "dark crimes and damnable transgressions of law" I have perpetrated.

Judge. That's so.

Hansell. And a "miscarriage of justice."

Judge. True again.

Hansell. All of which I brand as *infamous* lies!

Julius (*aside*) By golly, he's spunky!

Judge. (*irritated*) You do?

Hansell. Yes, sir. In the eye of the law a man is innocent until he is proved guilty.

Judge. Which *unfortunately* was not done in your case.

Hansell. Sir?

Judge. I mean what I say.

Hansell. To what do you refer?

Judge. I will tell you presently.

Hansell. I *demand* to know *now!*

Judge. (*rising angrily*) You do?

Hansell. Yes, sir!

Judge. Suppose I don't feel inclined to tell you?

Hansell. Then you are *no gentleman!*

JULIUS *notices* THOMAS *who beckons to him*—JULIUS *goes to him, they engage in earnest conversation*—THOMAS *places coin in* JULIUS' *hand; he examines it, places it in pants pocket and nods his head "yes."*

Judge. What?

Hansell. I mean what I say. What has changed your feeling toward me? But a few hours ago you believed me honest and worthy of your patronage, but *now*——

Judge. (*interrupting*) I know better; I have been duped by a petty adventurer, destitute of character.

Hansell. (*angrily*) Again I demand your proof!

Judge. (*warmly*) And you shall have it. Did you ever live in Swansville?

Hansell. I did.

Judge Why did you leave it?

Hansell. For reasons I beg to be excused from stating. (JULIUS *goes down* R.)

Judge. (*sneeringly*) Of course! Did you ever meet a young girl there by the name of Duer?

Hansell. Upon a number of occasions

Judge. (*significantly*) One of which you probably *well* remember!

Hansell. (*sadly*) Yes, too well!

Judge. (*significantly*) No doubt of it. What became of her?

Hansell. She was murdered.

Judge. By whom? (*watches him closely*)

Hansell. I do not know—that is, I am not positive.

Judge. (*knowingly*) You are not?

Hansell. No, sir.

Judge. Well, *I* know!

Hansell. You do?

Judge. Yes, sir!

Hansell. Who was it?

Judge. (*sneeringly*) A young man who has since assumed the rôle of a *gentlemanly* mechanic.

Hansell. His name?

Judge. Henry Hansell.

Hansell. '*Tis false!*

Thomas. (*springing from concealment; stands* R.) *It is true!*

Hansell. (*perceives* THOMAS; *starts*) Now I see! (*to* JUDGE) So he, (*pointing to* THOMAS) is my accuser?

Thomas. And an eye-witness of your crime.

Hansell. (*vehemently*) *You lie!*

Julius. (*quickly, aside*) Dat am puttin' it putty strong!

Judge. (*sternly*) Hansell, further denials are unnecessary. Your past career is well known to me, and the means you adopted to save your neck from a halter——

Hansell. (*interrupting*) But, sir——

Judge. Not a word. Your *crime* I have nothing to do with, but there is *another* matter which I *have*.

Hansell. (*quickly*) Don't trouble yourself to mention it—I accept no trust from a man who doubts my integrity. The position you offered me this morning is refused.

Judge. I was not referring to that.

Hansell. What then?

Judge. To your attentions to my ward, which, by the way, are as degrading to her, as your presumption is insulting to me.

Hansell. (*sneeringly*) Thank you!

Judge. (*angrily*) Young man, it ill becomes one in your position to assume an injured air.

Hansell. Enough of this, what are your wishes?

Judge. That you openly, before me, apologize to my ward for the degradation you have caused her, and sever all ties existing between you.

Hansell. That I will *never* do!

Judge. What?

Hansell. No, sir. If Miss Bell—(enter LAURA, C. D., *manifesting intense interest; quietly approaches back of* HANSELL) believes me capable of the sin *you* have charged me with, all she has to do is to say so, and we are parted; for I crave the love of *no woman* who has not implicit faith in the integrity of my character.

Laura. (*at* R. *of* HANSELL; *speaks warmly*) Most nobly spoken! *When* she doubts it, then will be the time for separation.

Judge. (*taken aback*) What, Laura, you here?

Laura. Yes, sir.

Judge. I did not send for you.

Laura. I am aware of it. Overhearing the demand you made upon Henry in reference to myself, I thought it time to interfere.

Judge. (*angrily*) Leave the room this instant!

Laura. Pardon me for refusing, but——

Judge. (*sternly, pointing to* C. D.) *Go!*

Laura. *I shall not.* I am no longer a child compelled to obey your every whim, but a *woman*, with a woman's heart and devotion that *defies* all commands intended to injure the man she loves!

Judge. You will be sorry for this!

Laura. Perhaps I may, but that does not deter me from performing my duty.

Judge. Have you more confidence in him—(*indicating* HANSELL) than you have in me?

Laura. No, not more, for all I am and have I owe to your kind guardianship.

Judge. Then leave this room.

Laura. I cannot and *will not*, until you *prove* to me that Henry is unworthy of the trust I have reposed in him.

Judge. And if I do?

Laura. He will then be as dead to me forever!

Judge. Very well, I will do it, and fulfill my promise made you this morning. That man—(*indicating* HANSELL) once loved a maiden as pure and guileless as yourself, who trusted him with all the fervor born of woman's first love. She thought the sun ne'er shone upon a nobler creature of her Maker's handicraft, and her daily duties were made lighter and her life better by the faith she reposed in the promises he had made her ; and yet, one night, for reasons known only to himself, he *murdered* that pure, trusting creature and threw her body into the sea to hide his crime.

Laura. (*slightly bewildered*) Who did ?

Judge. Why, that man, (*pointing to* HANSELL) who *professes* to love *you* as he did Lillian Duer.

Laura. Do—you mean—Henry—here ?

Judge. Yes. (*sneeringly*) Where are his " knightly plumes " now ?

Laura. I do not believe it. (*to* HANSELL) Is it true ?

Hansell. Not a word of it !

Judge. Of course he'd deny it, but Mr. Thomas, there, can vouch for its truth.

Thomas. Having been an *eye witness*, Miss Bell, of his dastardly deed, I most assuredly can.

Laura. (*passionately*) Henry, once for all, tell me *honestly* if this be true ! Do not mock me with *untruths*, for time must reveal all secrets. Tell the *truth* and let the consequences take care of themselves. Aye, upon my bended knees (*kneeling*) I plead for the *whole truth !*

Hansell. It is *not* true !

Laura. *Swear it*, by the love you bear your mother, the most sacred tie which binds you to earth.

Hansell. (*with uplifted hand*) I *swear* it ; 'tis *false*, every word of it !

Laura. (*rising*) Thank Heaven ! Now let come what will, I shall never doubt you, nor forget my plighted vows.

Judge. (*angrily to* HANSELL) You infamous scoundrel ! how *dare* you deceive that innocent girl by taking that oath ?

Hansell. " Deception " is an art never practised by me, and as to that "oath " a clear conscience, an honest heart and a sense of what is right, enable a man to *swear* to what is true.

Judge. (*furiously*) Away with you ! Leave my house, you canting hypocrite. Before to-morrow's sun sets, your heinous deed shall be known throughout the length and breadth of this town.

Hansell. (*pleading*) Judge, one word before I go—for *myself* I ask nothing—but I have a gray-haired mother at home. If you carry out your purpose, the blow will kill her. Do what you please to me, but, in mercy's name, spare her.

Judge. Did you *spare* the mother of your murdered victim ?

Hansell. I have murdered no one.

Judge. Have you *spared my* feelings by robbing me of my ward's affections ?

Hansell. I could not help that.

Judge. No, nor shall *I* spare *you* from being branded with the title you so richly deserve.

Enter MRS. HANSELL *and* DOLLY C. D.—MRS. H. *is dressed in dark clothing, has heavy black veil over features, comes* C., DOLLY *trying to restrain her, followed by* NEB *who stands up* C.

Mrs. H. (*with power*) Then I shall! (*all appear startled*)

Laura. (*surprised, to* MRS. H.) You here?

Judge. Who is that woman?

Hansell. My mother.

Judge. What is the meaning of *her* presence?

Hansell. I do not know. (LAURA *goes to* MRS. H.)

Judge. (*to* LAURA) Do you know *her*, too?

Laura. Yes, sir.

Mrs. H. (*to* JUDGE) And *you* do, also. (*throws back veil*)

Judge. (*starting back in surprise*) Do my eyes deceive me! Whom do I behold?

Mrs. H. (*quickly*) *Your wife*—the mother of your son (*indicating* DOLLY *and* HANSELL) and daughter!

Hansell. I *his* son!

Dolly. He *my* father!

Mrs. H. Yes, my children, he's your father.

Dolly. I'm sorry to hear it.

Hansell. (*bitterly*) Better I had never been born!

Judge. (*to* HANSELL) I can heartily echo that wish.

Mrs. H. (*to* JUDGE) My son showed me the letter you wrote him this morning. Knowing your nature I determined to reveal myself to you, hoping thereby to avert the blow you meditated against your own flesh and blood.

Judge. No injury I can do him can equal the blow he has dealt me. To be a felon's father is a *living death!*

Hansell. (*warmly*) In a few minutes I shall leave your house, never to enter it again. (*to* MRS. H.) Mother, am I that man's son? (*pointing to* JUDGE)

Mrs. H. You are.

Hansell. His lawful son?

Mrs. H. Certainly.

Hansell. Then why am *I* called Hansell?

Mrs. H. Because, when I left your father's house, I adopted my mother's maiden name to prevent my retreat being discovered.

Laura. Now I know *why* you always wore that veil over your face when in public. It was done to prevent your husband from recognizing you.

Mrs. H. True, my child. Ever since I entered this town, the

abode of my husband, I have been in mortal terror lest he should discover who I was.

Laura. Why did you come here if you desired not to meet him ?

Mrs. H. Because Henry could obtain work nowhere else at the time. The firm he was employed by in Swansville failed, and as Dolly and I were dependent upon his exertions for our daily bread, it was come *here* or starve.

Judge. (*significantly*) Was that the only reason that brought you here ?

Mrs. H. (*haughtily*) It was.

Judge. I have heard a different story.

Hansell. (*hotly*) Be careful, sir, she is my mother and the only father I ever knew ! Insult her by what you contemplate, and as sure as there is a Heaven above I will resent it.

Mrs. H. Hush, Henry ! You'll do nothing of the kind. I came here expressly to plead in your behalf and expect to hear some bitter words. I wish to clear you in your father's eyes of all shadow of crime.

Hansell. Your mission will then be fruitless, for——

Mrs. H. Hush ! I know what you were going to say, but I do not believe it. (*to* JUDGE) You believe Henry to be a criminal?

Judge. I do.

Mrs. H. Are you aware that he was tried and acquitted ?

Judge. I am, and also what *means* were used to accomplish that purpose.

Mrs. H. I do not understand to what you refer ?

Judge. (*curtly*) *Perjured evidence!*

Mrs. H. Explain yourself.

Judge. Was he not acquitted by the evidence of yourself and your daughter?

Mrs. H. He was.

Judge. By your sworn testimony that he never left his home the evening of the murder?

Mrs. H. Yes.

Judge. Were you not aware when you testified to that fact that it was *false?*

Mrs. H. (*in surprise*) What do you mean?

Judge. That he *did* leave his home, and that you *knew* it.

Mrs. H. No, I was not aware of that fact, neither is it true.

Hansell. (*quickly, with eagerness*) Mother, do you really mean that ?

Mrs. H. I *do.* It is the truth.

Hansell. (*with feeling*) At last peace has been found. Pardon me for doubting you, but I have always thought you knew of my absence, but *believing* in my *innocence* testified as you did to save me from the gallows.

Mrs. H. My son, *how could* you ever believe me guilty of such a crime?

Hansell. I know *now* how unjustly I have wronged you, and beg your forgiveness.

Thomas. Judge, why pursue this matter further? He has confessed his guilt by acknowledging his absence from his home the night of the murder.

Hansell. (*angrily to* THOMAS) Suggestions from *you* are not required, and I have confessed nothing that implicates me in any crime.

Thomas. Haven't you? Do you deny seeing Lillian Duer the night of her murder?

Hansell. *Alive?* Yes.

Thomas. Dead?

Hansell. No.

Thomas. You were seen bending over her form.

Hansell. I am aware of that—by *you.*

Thomas. Yes, and by *some one* else.

Hansell. (*surprised*) Who?

Thomas. By Julius there.

Judge. If you are innocent as you claim, explain what you were doing when seen by Mr. Thomas.

Hansell. I was probably examining the body, to see if I could identify it.

Thomas. (*sneeringly*) A likely story!

Judge. What excuse have you to offer for leaving your home at that particular time?

Hansell. (*significantly*) Suppose you ask Thomas there the same question.

Thomas. That's unnecessary; besides, I can make a satisfactory answer.

Judge. I addressed my request to you—will you answer?

Hansell. I will, but I do not expect you to believe me. I was simply taking a walk.

Judge. For what purpose?

Hansell. To obtain comfort. The heat in my bedroom was so oppressive I could not rest; so I rose, dressed myself and was walking along the beach, when I came across the body of her whose life you accuse me of taking.

Judge. Well—proceed.

Hansell. Stooping down, I examined it and found it to be the lifeless form of my old playmate. I then—(*brokenly*) Excuse me from saying anything more, excepting that I returned home horror-stricken. (*averts head; appearance of sadness*)

Thomas. (*smiles knowingly*) Adroitly explained, Judge. Corroborates my statement to a nicety!

Judge. True !

Thomas. (*pointing exultingly*) Look at him ! Has he the appearance of an innocent man ? Do you longer doubt his guilt ?

Judge. No, nor can any one else.

Laura. (*quickly*) Well, *I* do. Shame upon you both for your lack of charity.

Judge. Laura, do you still believe in his innocence after what you have heard ?

Laura. *I do*, and ever shall believe him what I do now—a pure, noble, innocent man. And all you two may *do* and *say* will never shake my faith in his declarations.

Julius. (*quickly, aside*) Bully fur her !

Judge. He is my son ; would to Heaven I had your confidence. I would gladly share your belief, but when I remember that Mr. Thomas saw him commit his foul deed, I cannot.

Mrs. H. (*agitated*) Henry, is that so ?

Hansell. (*quickly*) As God is my witness—it is not !

Thomas. (*excitedly to* HANSELL) I *saw* you commit the deed.

Hansell. (*with warmth*) You did not !

Thomas. I did, and can prove by Julius, here, that I did.

Hansell. What does *he* know about the affair ?

Julius. Heaps mor'n yo' s'pose.

Thomas. He was a witness of your act.

Julius. Yes, dat's so.

Thomas. (*exultingly*) Now, are *all* satisfied ?

Laura. No, sir, I'm *not !*

Thomas. (*quickly*) Then you *shall* be. Julius, didn't you see Miss Duer strangled ?

Julius. Yes, sah.

Thomas. And didn't that man (*pointing to* HANSELL) perform the deed ?

Julius. (*emphatically*) No, sah, he didn't.

Thomas. (*excitedly*) What !

Julius. No, sah ; yo' did it yo'se'f.

Thomas. (*drawing knife and springing at* JULIUS) You lying scoundrel ! I'll cut your throat——

Julius. (*quickly drawing horse pistol and covering* THOMAS) No, yo' won't, fur I'll let daylight fro' yo' fust. (THOMAS *stops*—MRS. H. *and* LAURA *slightly retreat* L., *alarmed*) Yo' tho't I only seed Massa Henry dar dat night, but I seed yo' kill dat gal afore he cum, an' hide ahind de rocks. (THOMAS *starts for* JULIUS) Stop, or I'll pull on yo' fur sartin.

Thomas. Curse you, you shall pay dearly for your treachery !

Julius. P'raps I may, but not in dis world if I'se knows myse'f.

Laura. (*to* JUDGE) Have him arrested !

Thomas. (*starting quickly for* C. D.) I'll not be taken alive !

Judge. (*loudly*) Stop him! Stop him!

Neb. (*excitedly, as* THOMAS *passes him*) Pull on him, Jule, pull on him! (*as* THOMAS *reaches* C. D. *he is met by* HANS ; *they collide—* THOMAS *sends* HANS *sprawling* R. *and rushes out* L.—NEB *follows him out*)

Julius. (*replacing pistol*) Let him go, he'll not git furder dan de front door, fur I'se got a perlice dar to 'rest him.

Judge. (*to* JULIUS) How is that?

Julius. Why, you see, I 'tended to blow on him, anyhow, 'kase he wus a gittin too ind'pendent an' sassy-like fur me. He 'tended not to know a feller when he met me on de street. So when I seed him cum in here, knowin' he wus workin' agin' Massa Henry dar, I jist scooted out an' posted de perlice to watch de doors an' not let him 'scape.

Laura. (*to* JUDGE) I can't conceive how you allowed yourself to be imposed upon by that man Thomas!

Judge. It is a mystery to me, also. I shall never forgive myself for the injustice done my *own* flesh and blood. (*pistol shots heard off back*) What's that?

Julius. Oh, I guess de perlice am a gibin' Thomas a dose ob pills to swaller.

Hansell. (*to* JULIUS) How came you in Swansville? (MRS. H. *crosses to* DOLLY. *and they engage in earnest conversation*)

Julius. I used ter lib dar, 'fore I took sarvice wid de Jedge.

Hansell. Then why didn't you come forward at my trial and expose Thomas?

Julius. Kase it wus no use, you got free any how ; 'sides I wus 'fraid Thomas might (*imitates throttling*) me. He nebber knowed I seed *him* kill de gal. Yo' see, I wus a comin' home frum a coon hunt, when all ob a sudden I came across Thomas an' a gal quarrelin'. I got 'hind a tree to see de fun. Dey wus bofe mad as fire. Thomas wanted de gal to promise him sumfin' an' she wouldn't, so he chokes her. Den I 'spects he seed yo' comin' down de beach, kase he got 'hind some rocks an' hid. Putty soon yo' cum 'long, 'zamined de gal, muttered sumfin' sort o' mournful like an' went away.

Hansell. And Thomas, what did he do then?

Julius. He cotched sight ob me, so he cum right ober to whar I wus—I wus skeered so bad I couldn't run. He grabs me by de neck an' says, "'Member, if yo's am called 'pon, dat dat man," pointing to yo', " killed dat gal." I said " all right." He gib me sum money an' went away. I don't know how *I* got home.

Hansell. If you were in league with Thomas, why didn't he call you to strengthen his testimony at my trial.

Julius. I dunno, guess he wus 'fraid I knowed mor'n I 'tended to. He of'en axed me 'bout de matter when I tackled him fur money, but I nebber gave him any satisfaction. But I allus got my money all de same.

Enter NEB *excitedly*, C. D.

Neb. De perlice am got him now, but dey hab to shoot him fust, he fit like a wild cat. (*stands* L. *of* MRS. H.)

Mrs. H. Poor man, I pity him!

Judge. Pity is wasted upon a man of his brutal instincts. Let us rather hope he will repent of his misdeeds before his day of reckoning comes. (*to* HANSELL) Henry, I feel it is almost like adding insult to injury to ask your forgiveness for the harsh treatment you have received from me.

Hansell. (*interrupting*) You could not well do otherwise, for appearances certainly were against me.

Judge. Yet they should not have influenced me, after your repeated declarations of innocence. There (*extending hand*) is my hand. Let not your duty as a *son* sway you one iota, but if as a *man* you will accept it, I solemnly promise to make you what atonement lies in my power.

Hansell. I accept it, both as a *man* and a *son*, desiring nothing more but justice for my mother and sister.

Judge. That *both* shall have. The past has taught me a lesson I shall never forget. My house, fortune, *all* I possess, is theirs to command.

Dolly. (*quickly*) Which would be worthless to us unless you shared it.

Judge. (*sadly*) That cannot be. My transgressions against your mother are too great ever for me to obtain pardon.

Dolly. Ask and——

Mrs. H. (*interrupting*) No, no—do not urge that *now*. Let us return to our humble home and resume our old ways. If in the future a reconciliation is considered best for the advancement of your interests, my dear children, I will gladly forget my past sufferings and do all in *my* power to effect it.

Hansell. Nobly spoken, mother. That ensures us a reunited family in the near future.

Judge. Then with Laura for your wife, your name at the head of our firm, and my dear wife once more sharing our happiness——

Dolly. (*interrupting*) And *I* to train *you*——

Judge. (*smiling*) There will be nothing but sunshine to make glad our remaining days.

Julius. (*dolefully*) May I ax wot yo' 'tend to do wid me an' Neb?

Judge. Why, I thought you both were going to leave me.

Julius. Well, we might stay wid yo' if yo' 'suaded us hard 'nough.

Judge. That will depend upon your future conduct.

Neb. All right, den we'll be a part ob de great Buttons family.

JUDGE *down* R. C.; HANSELL *and* LAURA *down* L. C.; MRS. HANSELL R. C., *back of* JUDGE; DOLLY L. C., *back of* HANSELL *and* LAURA; JULIUS *down* R. *of* JUDGE; NEB *up* C.; HANS *in* dvorway C.

CURTAIN—QUICK DROP.

www.ingramcontent.com/pod-product-compliance
Lightning Source LLC
Chambersburg PA
CBHW030024030726
47499CB00008B/3113